FANGS & FICTION

A LIBRARY WITCH MYSTERY

ELLE ADAMS

1

"Okay, library," I said, facing the balconies overlooking the ground floor. "Activate normal mode."

I wrote the word *move* in the notebook in my hand, focusing on the shelves in front of me. Yet no matter how hard I focused, the library remained the same—five storeys of towering shelves tiered like the layers on a wedding cake, complete with floating lanterns, temperamental staircases, and books that did whatever they pleased.

Most of the time, the library felt like the home I'd always yearned for. For as long as I could remember, I'd sought comfort in the old-book smell of leather tomes and the fresh scent of printed pages, and I'd settled into life in my family's magical library as though I'd never been anywhere else. Yet it seemed I had a long way to go before the library was open to obeying my commands like it did for my other family members.

"What in the world are you doing?" My cousin Cass walked into view, accompanied by her sister, Estelle.

"Laney is supposed to be coming here tomorrow," I explained. "I thought I'd get the library prepared for her."

"You invited your non-magical friend to visit the library?" Cass arched a brow. "You might as well have invited a sheep to have dinner with a pack of wolves."

"Nobody's getting eaten," I said firmly. "Besides, the library does have a 'normal' mode. Aunt Adelaide told me."

"We haven't used it in years." Cass tugged her long, curly red hair into a ponytail, which contrasted her sister's flowing curls. She was taller and leaner than her sister and wore glasses, but the three of us looked alike enough that Laney would know we were related the instant she set eyes on my cousins. "Estelle, you can't seriously be thinking of going along with this ridiculous idea."

"Look, Rory's friend wants to visit her," said Estelle. "Rory has done so much for us since she moved in, and the least we can do is give her that."

In truth, I was having second thoughts on the matter myself. While I'd longed to invite my best friend Laney to visit my new family from the first day I'd moved to the library, the magical laws forbade normals like her from entering the paranormal world. And that wasn't even getting into the fact that most ordinary people would run screaming if they wandered into certain sections of the library, where magical beasts lurked in the stacks and the books often got into fights with one another. She knew I'd recently gone to live with some newly discovered relatives in their library, but not the *magic* part of it.

"It's her funeral if we all get arrested." Cass's pessimism was hardly new. She was not a fan of meeting new people, unless they came with feathers or fangs.

"We won't," Estelle said. "We had a normal living here in the library for years without anyone kicking up a fuss. None of the local officials from the witch council ever check up on Ivory Beach."

"Exactly," I said, remembering poor Tad, a normal who'd once made his home in the Reading Corner after his first glimpse of the magical world had driven him out of his mind. As my family's library was the centre of the town rather than a ruling coven under the thumb of the local witch council, the laws were a little laxer in the town of Ivory Beach than they were in other paranormal communities. That didn't mean inviting Laney to visit couldn't go wrong in a hundred possible ways, though. While my best friend was resilient and open-minded, she'd never seen anything more magical than a Harry Potter movie or Disneyland.

My own introduction to the magical world had come with a fair few bumps. My dad, who I'd always thought of as ordinary, had left the magical world behind to marry my mother and kept his secret until his death three years prior. As a result, I hadn't even known I had any surviving family until they'd showed up a few months ago to help me deal with a group of vampires at the bookshop where I—and my dad, before he'd died—had worked.

My induction to the paranormal world had been so abrupt that I'd had to leave Laney behind, and I wanted to give her an insight into my new life, even an incomplete one. The library, however, was excessive even by paranormal standards, containing an entire corridor which had turned invisible, a Dimensional Studies Section which moved around as it pleased, and a vampire sleeping in the basement who'd been there since before I was born.

As if to highlight my misgivings, a muffled crash came from upstairs, and a handful of tawny feathers drifted down over the balcony along with a sprinkle of glitter. With a groan, I went in search of the trouble and found myself in the middle of yet another standoff between a pixie and an owl. Supervised, as usual, by a crow.

Spark the pixie, his eight-inch-tall frame dressed in a miniature suit, flitted around on gossamer wings, avoiding the sharp talons of the huge tawny owl who served as my family's familiar. Sylvester flew in gleeful circles, swatting at his target, while my own familiar, Jet, watched from the side lines. The little crow usually went against taking sides most of the time, instead flying around shrieking and adding to the general clamour.

"They're fighting!" he told me in his squeaky voice.

"I know." I reached out to catch the pixie and then withdrew my hand sharply before it ended up caught in one of the owl's sharp talons. "Sylvester, cut it out."

He ignored me, diving at the pixie with a screech that raised the hairs on my arms. Jet hid himself in the folds of my silver-lined black cloak, while the pixie shot into the air like a glittering bullet to avoid the owl's claws.

"Sylvester!" I said, louder. "What's going on?"

"He dropped glitter in my feathers!" said Sylvester indignantly.

"Not on purpose." I caught sight of the pixie zipping around above, shedding glitter as he did so. The stuff got everywhere, but I doubted the pixie had been the aggressor. "Right, Spark?"

The pixie made an unintelligible noise, flitting down to perch on Estelle's shoulder as she caught me up.

Sylvester hovered above us like a feathery demon. "He did it on purpose. Ask him."

"Calm down." Estelle raised her hands placatingly and turned to the pixie perching on her shoulder. Spark chattered in her ear, and Estelle narrowed her eyes at the owl. "Sylvester, he says you put a dead mouse in his nest. Really?"

"It's a lie!" Sylvester said in outraged tones. "The little toadstool has it in for me."

"You've done nothing but pick fights with him ever since he moved in," Estelle said. "Cass, back me up here."

Her sister gave a shrug. "Sylvester's right to be annoyed. He does leave glitter everywhere."

"And the dead mouse?" I arched a brow at the owl.

"There was no mouse!" Sylvester said.

"There's a simple way to verify that." Estelle raised her wand and marched across the lobby towards the stairs. The pixie, after being chased off by several of the books, had opted to make his nest in an alcove up on the first floor. "I take it I won't find any mice up there?"

Sylvester cleared his throat. "I *may* have found a small rodent sniffing around the stacks and put it in the general vicinity of where that glitter-shedding cretin makes his nest."

"Really." Estelle turned on her heel, folding her arms in disapproval. "You're better than that, Sylvester."

"She's right." Even if he *was* jealous of the pixie for monopolising our attention lately, you'd think the living embodiment of the library's entire store of knowledge would have better things to do than get into ridiculous fights.

"You're all ganging up on me." The owl took flight with a piercing shriek that caused several books to leap off the shelves in fright. Estelle made an exasperated noise and went to restore them to their former places, the pixie still clinging to her cloak. As Jet took flight in pursuit of the owl, I moved in to help her.

"Maybe this wasn't such a good idea," Estelle said. The pixie was supposed to be her charge, but while he'd got the hang of being her assistant quickly enough, Sylvester had made it his full-time mission to drive the pixie off. Admittedly, the pixie still turned invisible occasionally and dropped glitter all over everything, but the main issue was on Sylvester's end. And since he wasn't a normal owl in any way, it was hard for us to reason with him.

I waved my wand at the books that had fallen to the floor, and they flew back to their rightful positions. Estelle gave me a grateful look, while Cass scoffed from behind us. "Now there's glitter on the books, too. Are you sure you want to invite your friend here now, Rory?"

Not in the slightest. Laney and I had been trying to make plans for weeks, but something always came up. Between lessons on biblio-witch magic, spellwork, potion-making, wrangling my familiar and magical theory, my days were full enough without adding the complication of juggling my old life with my new one.

"Is that a no?" said Cass. "Why not just ask that Reaper of yours to come with you to meet her somewhere else?"

For once, Cass wasn't trying to needle me on purpose. Xavier wanted to come with me to meet Laney, but there were difficulties. Namely, with his boss. "I would, but the

Grim Reaper doesn't like him going outside of his designated area."

"He doesn't get to leave the town at all?" Estelle asked.

"Not unless the Grim Reaper takes him to one of those mysterious Reaper meetings." I sighed. "I'm sure he sneaks off sometimes. It's just whether he can get away with going on a day trip with me without his boss flipping out and thinking he's ditched his post."

"The guy needs to chill," said Cass. "Why not slip him a sleeping potion?"

Estelle choked. "Cass, he's the Grim Reaper. Unless you want to hasten your path to an early grave, I wouldn't slip him anything."

"I meant without being seen, of course," said Cass.

"The Grim Reaper can sense you even if you're invisible, according to Xavier," I said. "No potion or spell has any effect on him, besides."

"Pity," said Cass. "So he did tell you some of his secrets, then. Has he told you about his family yet?"

I gave her a warning look. "Cass, I'm entertaining Laney as a guest, not the Reaper. Besides, that line of questioning is closed."

Maybe it was for the best that we met up outside the library after all, since I didn't want Laney to be subject to an interrogation the way poor Xavier had the one time he'd come for dinner with my family. Admittedly, Laney worked as an assistant in the local supermarket, which provided fewer openings for my family to ask her nosy questions which might lead to the Grim Reaper showing up on our doorstep. Didn't mean I wouldn't stand up for her if necessary.

Laughter trickled from behind a nearby bookshelf,

and Aunt Candace came into view with her notebook and pen at the ready. If I had to guess, she'd been watching the fight between the pixie and the owl. Her wild curly hair was barely restrained, her cloak covered in coffee stains, and her eyes alight with mischief.

"What?" I said to her. "What's so funny?"

"You," she said. "You're really expecting the library to behave itself? Please bring the normal here. I'm writing another paranormal-normal romance and I need ideas."

"Nice try." I narrowed my eyes at her quivering pen and notebook. "You're not allowed to put my friends into books if they don't know you're a writer."

"That's the best way to do it," she said. "No potential for lawsuits whatsoever."

Honestly. Leaving my aunt cackling to herself, I scanned the upper balconies for any signs of Aunt Adelaide and instead spotted someone else entirely gliding through the stacks.

Evangeline, the leader of the vampires in town, walked out from behind a row of bookshelves, clothed in an elegant black dress that matched the waterfall of silky hair that framed her narrow, chalk-pale face. The vampire descended the stairs with speed no human could match, somehow avoiding all the trick stairs in the process. Though maybe even the trick stairs were frightened of her. It wouldn't surprise me. I hadn't even seen her come in. More importantly, had she heard our conversation about inviting Laney to come to town? *I hope not.*

Even if she hadn't, vampires could read minds, and I was too startled to shield when she gave me a wide smile. "It's an honour to see you, Aurora."

"What are you doing in here?" The way she'd sneaked

in while none of us was looking set alarm bells ringing in my mind, and I fixed my attention on a wooden bannister to avoid any wayward thoughts slipping out.

"Why, nothing at all." Her gaze panned around the shelves. "I heard you had a pixie on your staff now."

"We do. He's our new assistant." I glanced at Estelle behind me, seeing the pixie had hidden himself behind her hair. "Is there something I can help you with? Are you looking for a particular book?"

"No, I don't think I am." She crossed the lobby to the door with elegant steps, her dress flowing around her ankles. "You have glitter in your hair, by the way."

"I know." I'd learnt to shield my mind from her via focusing on one particular thing to the exclusion of everything else, but stray thoughts could still slip out if I wasn't careful, and it took a great effort for me to suppress the impulse to check my dad's journal was still in my bag. It wouldn't be the first time she'd shown an interest in getting her hands on it, and I couldn't think of any other reason for her to come to the library if not to take out a book. Evangeline wasn't the type to pay social calls, and the vampires' leader wasn't my biggest fan for multiple reasons, the most recent of which was the fact that she thought the fact that I was dating Xavier meant I'd picked the Grim Reaper's side over hers.

I couldn't say I knew the details of the vampires' odd rivalry with the Reapers. Unlike the vampires and the werewolves, they didn't tend to get into public fights, they just avoided one another. I half expected her to turn back and offer an explanation, even a cryptic one, but she reached the doors and vanished through them without looking back.

"That was weird," I commented. At least the pixie hadn't dropped glitter in her hair, as he'd done to the rest of us.

Aunt Adelaide walked into view. "What did she want?"

"Nothing, apparently," I said. "Who let her in?"

"I turned my back for five minutes." She shook her head. "Strange creatures, vampires."

I opened my shoulder bag to make sure the journal was still there, a faded leather-bound book filled with writing I couldn't read. Nor could anyone else, including my Aunt Adelaide's homemade translator spell. I'd never found the original code-breaker document, so I'd been unable to figure out just *why* every vampire I met seemed determined to get their hands on it.

According to my aunts' research, the journal was of interest to a particular group of vampires who collected rare artefacts, and while their leader, Mortimer Vale, was currently in jail, two of his companions were at large. Evangeline might not be in league with them, but I'd been warned against showing her the journal all the same. All I knew was that it contained some kind of knowledge considered valuable to the vampires, but translating it seemed as likely as my family and their familiars remaining on their best behaviour for the duration of a visit from my best friend.

On cue, my phone buzzed with a message from Laney: *Where is this elusive boyfriend of yours?*

He's around. He has a demanding job.

Namely, taking the dead into the afterlife. Which was as demanding as you could get. No excuses, no days off, and a boss who happened to be the literal Grim Reaper. It was a miracle we'd made our relationship work at all. But

Xavier was possibly the least likely person to cause trouble for her during our visit.

I sent her another message: *Also, my family is having a demanding time at the library, so we might have to meet elsewhere. That okay?*

Her response came a moment later. *Why don't you come home?*

I hesitated, then replied, *Bad memories.*

What, of me?

No. Abe. My old employer was nothing compared to the vampires who'd cost me my job, but that didn't mean I was keen to relive that time in my life, either.

On the other hand, going back to my old home was one way to ensure Laney could meet Xavier without accidentally glimpsing the magical world.

Ah. Understandable. Still, you don't have to talk to that miserable old git. Come see me.

I'll check with Xavier.

"Messaging your friend?" Aunt Adelaide guessed. "I heard you trying to get the library to switch into normal mode earlier. Truth be told, I'm not certain it's possible to hide every trace of magic in here, and then there's our visitors to consider. We can't ask everyone in town to refrain from using magic at all."

True. Even if Laney visited on a Sunday when the library was closed, it'd be just my luck if we ran into a magical duel between two angry witches in the middle of town or a werewolf breaking the 'no shifting in public' rule.

"It's okay," I said. "I think we're going to meet up back where I used to live instead. That is, if the Grim Reaper lets Xavier come with me without kicking up a fuss. I'll ask him now so he can give the boss enough time to prepare."

I sent him a quick text, and a moment later, there came a knock on the door. The Reaper was nothing if not prompt.

"Hey." I opened the door to find Xavier standing on the doorstep. His blond curly hair and aquamarine eyes were the antithesis of what one would expect the Grim Reaper to look like, but then again, looking like an angel probably helped him when it came to escorting reluctant souls into the afterworld. "Change of plans. We're meeting Laney back home in my old town, if you can get permission from you-know-who."

"She's not coming here?"

"Nope. Too much madness." I took his hand. "I can't get the library to behave itself, and Sylvester is still feuding with that pixie. Will your boss give you permission to leave town for an hour or two, or will we have to sneak out and hope he doesn't notice?"

He tilted his head. "I'm still free during that time. If I tell him we're going for a walk in the hills and will still be within sight of the town, he won't know any better. Granted, if it goes wrong, he's likely to be furious, but that won't happen unless I give him reason to suspect my absence."

"Okay." I nodded. "As a bonus, you'll get to see where I grew up."

"I take it we're going there via magical means?" he said.

"You bet." I started typing a reply to Laney. "I haven't used a spell to travel that far before, but I don't think I could go back to public transport now."

"Good, because I suspect my boss will have words to

say to me if I use my Reaper powers to travel to the normal world," he commented.

"Especially as you aren't supposed to be leaving town." My heart gave an uneasy flip. Deceiving the Grim Reaper was not wise. I'd been lucky to keep my head the last time I'd done it. "Better hope nobody dies while we're gone."

With luck, I wasn't tempting fate.

2

I woke bright and early the following morning, prepared for a trip down memory lane. Or as prepared as it was possible to get, anyway. I opted to wear ordinary jeans and a jacket, leaving my cloak behind. I did carry my Biblio-Witch Inventory, pen and notebook in my shoulder bag along with my wand, though. With luck, I wouldn't need them.

My heart flipped with nerves as I waited for Xavier to show up at the door. Prompt as usual, he knocked, and I greeted him with a wan smile.

"I told my boss we're going out walking in the hills," he said. "He won't check up on me."

"If you're sure." I took in a breath. "Ready for this?"

"I am," he said.

I'm not sure I *am.* But Laney was expecting me, and I wouldn't let her down.

I crossed the library to the desk and opened my Biblio-Witch Inventory, then I tapped the word *travel.* In my mind's eye, I pictured the town I'd grown up in. I could only use that spell to travel to places I'd already been, but it wasn't hard to conjure up a mental image of the street where I'd once worked, or the river, where three vampires had chased me—

The two of us vanished from the library, and then reappeared an instant later on a street which ran alongside a river.

Déjà-vu rushed over me. I hadn't wanted to picture this street when I'd used the spell, but it'd lurked in the back of my mind all the same. From this view, the world behind hadn't changed an inch since I'd left. I could even see my old apartment block in the distance. Someone else would live in my old flat now. Someone who would have no idea the magical world existed alongside this one.

The uneasy, out-of-time feeling intensified, as though I watched my previous self through a window. When I'd last been here, I'd assumed I'd had no family left, my job had been a dead end, and I'd believed, deep down, that nobody would miss me if I left.

Except, that is, for one person.

"Rory!" Laney waved furiously at me from the bridge, wearing a thick coat with a long rainbow-striped scarf wrapped around her neck. "You were totally spaced out."

"Yeah. I guess I was." I ran over to hug her. "It's great to see you."

"You, too." She hugged me back, her mouth stretched in a grin. She'd cut her long curly brown hair since I'd left so it bounced to shoulder-length, topped with a woollen hat. "And… this is Xavier?"

"I am," he said. "It's great to meet you."

"Wow." She blinked at him, her eyes rounding as they took in the improbable appearance of a blond Reaper with aquamarine eyes. At least the scythe he carried strapped to his back was invisible to her.

I cleared my throat. "Should we walk?"

We headed away from the bridge and toward the high street. I fell into step with Laney along the way, and I poked her in the arm, whispering, "Stop staring."

"Sorry," she whispered back. "But you know, I don't even like guys in that way and I think he's gorgeous. I hope his personality matches his face."

Heat crept up my neck and I averted my gaze. "It does, don't worry."

"Good." A bounce entered her step. "I'm happy for you."

My worries faded a little, and despite the seemingly endless length of time since we'd last seen one another, it was easy to fall back into familiar patterns. Xavier was as charming as ever, and even if Laney hadn't been enamoured with his appearance, his easy humour would have won her over anyway. We spent a couple of hours wandering up and down the high street before ducking into a café to warm up with hot chocolate and cakes. Everything seemed to be going well, while the magical world remained tucked away into a corner of my mind. The notion of keeping my two lives separate didn't seem so far-fetched after all.

At least until we left the café and walked back down the high street towards the bridge over the river. Out of the corner of my eye, I spotted a tall figure on the bridge, clad in black and looking out across the water. My heart gave a lurch and I stopped in my tracks, my gaze jumping to the bridge.

The stranger was no longer there.

Maybe I'd imagined him out of a sudden spate of jumpiness brought on by being so close to the scene of my first encounter with the dangers of the magical world… but how could I be certain?

Laney shot me a quizzical look. "Something wrong?"

"No, just thought I saw…" I trailed off, less certain by the second. It might have been some ordinary bystander. No use in worrying Laney over nothing. "Abe. I doubt it was him, though. He wouldn't leave the bookshop during a workday."

"Oh, him." She wrinkled her nose. "Not that I blame you for working at that shop for so many years, but you're well shot of him. You deserve better."

"Agreed," Xavier put in.

"I'm glad you found the library instead," Laney added. "It's perfect for you. I can't believe your other family members didn't contact you before."

I gave an uncomfortable shrug. "They fell out of touch with my dad before he died."

Laney studied my face. "Didn't they know… I mean, they knew he died, right?"

"They did," I said, doing my best to stick to the truth as far as possible, "but they didn't know if I'd want to get in touch with them or not. I mean, they'd never met me before in my life. I was a stranger to them."

Not a lie, but my words brought a fresh wave of gratitude towards my aunts and cousins for what they'd given me. A second chance to make something of my life, and a home more welcoming than any I'd had since I'd lost my parents.

"I'm glad they found you, then," said Laney. "Where are you going?"

I'd unconsciously turned to the right, down the street adjacent to the river. "Just seeing if it's still there."

Laney understood my meaning without me having to say so aloud, and she and Xavier followed behind me until I came to a halt, feeling a cold fist clench around my heart.

There it was. Abe's bookshop. It was still in business, for a wonder, though I knew from our records last year that we'd barely been scraping by. Even before I'd worked there full-time, the bookshop had always been a fixture in my life. Dad had been devoted to it, and it had broken my heart to see Abe let his business crumble one brick at a time. Not deliberately—the place opened every day, rain or shine, holidays or otherwise, and Abe only begrudgingly closed the shop for Christmas. Still, he'd always rejected all my ideas to help us attract more customers. I wondered if he'd found anyone else willing to help him out.

I took a step back from the window as someone approached the display, carefully arranging a stack of books. Abe must have hired a new assistant. A teenage girl, by the look of things, who wore the same uniform I had when I'd worked there, drab clothes which had always made me look older than my age. Considering he'd pretty much told me he couldn't afford an assistant at all when he'd fired me, I'd bet he paid her less than he'd paid me. Poor thing.

I turned my back on my replacement and walked away, feeling slightly dazed. Between Abe's new employee and the man I thought I'd seen near the river, I'd had quite enough ventures down memory lane for one day.

"You're better off without that job in your life," Laney told me. "Trust me. Are you heading home now?"

"Sure, we're getting the train." An easy enough cover story—provided she didn't see us vanish into thin air, anyway. "I'll be back to see you again before you know it."

"Or I can always come and visit you. You aren't getting rid of me that easily." She hugged me goodbye. "What did you say the name of your town was again, Ivory Beach?"

Uh-oh. Had I let the name slip without realising? "I don't remember saying."

"You mentioned it in one of your texts," she said. "It's cool. I'll warn you before I come and stalk you."

She waved goodbye one last time and then walked away, back up the high street. I watched her go, nostalgia tugging at my heart. "This was a good idea. Coming here, I mean."

"I'm glad," said Xavier. "Not that I didn't want her to come to Ivory Beach, but I think asking the library to be on its best behaviour is a bit of a stretch. And your family."

"Not to mention there's no danger of the Grim Reaper showing up out here." I cast another glance up the high street and saw Laney had disappeared among the crowd of shoppers. "I suppose there's no danger of her accidentally stumbling across the town, since it's magically hidden from any regular maps."

I turned back to the bridge and my heart gave a thump when I saw the same shadowy figure I'd seen earlier, too far away to make out his features.

"Rory?" Xavier followed my gaze. "What...?"

"Did you see someone over there? A tall man, wearing black?"

"Let me see." He set off in a blur, faster than regular

human speed, then zipped back to my side. "Nobody we know."

Meaning, nobody magical. "Maybe I'm losing my grip. I mean, this bridge is where the vampires cornered me."

Xavier's eyes widened. "Wait, is this where you were attacked? You should have said, and we'd have met Laney somewhere else."

"It's fine," I lied. "Besides, it was on my mind, so blame my subconscious for bringing us here."

"Well, there's nobody here now." His warm, steady gaze grounded me. "You're safe."

"I know." With a quick glance up the high street to ensure Laney was out of sight, I pulled out my Biblio-Witch Inventory, tapped the word *travel,* and pictured the library as vividly as I could manage.

Xavier and I vanished, and then we reappeared a moment later on the library doorstop. Close enough. I caught my balance against the door, putting my Biblio-Witch Inventory back into my pocket.

"Nicely done." Xavier wrapped me into his warm embrace—warmer than any Reaper had the right to be— and kissed me goodbye. "Better make sure my boss hasn't reaped any souls in my absence."

I hope that was a joke. Deceiving the Reaper wasn't done lightly, but I couldn't bring myself to regret our excursion today.

As Xavier turned to leave, the library door opened, and Aunt Adelaide appeared in the doorway. "Oh, you're back. Hello, Rory. And... is Xavier still there?"

"Yes." He turned to her with a quizzical look. "I'm still here. Is something wrong?"

"I thought you'd have been called back right away," said Aunt Adelaide.

"Why?" I looked between them. "What did I miss?"

"They pulled a body out of the river on the town's boundary," she explained.

Xavier's eyes widened. "They did? I didn't sense anything..."

But of course he wouldn't. Ordinarily, if someone died, Xavier was called to their side by a magical force known only to the Grim Reaper himself. He had no choice in the matter.

Yet someone had died while we were gone... but Xavier hadn't been called out to collect their soul.

Oh, no.

"I'll check," he said. "My boss might have dealt with the victim himself."

Or he might have gone looking for us and found us missing. But Xavier had told his boss he was going to be out with me today, so that ought to mean the Grim Reaper should have gone in his place. Right?

If not... we might be in trouble.

———

I didn't sleep much that night, and I rose for my magic lesson the following morning feeling like I'd need to take a bath in a vat of coffee before I'd be ready for the day ahead. I settled for grabbing a mug from the kitchen to bring with me to the classroom where I usually took my lessons.

Aunt Candace apparently wasn't prepared for the

morning either, because she'd left Estelle sitting in her place.

"Hey, Rory," she said. "Aunt Candace is at a tricky stage in her manuscript, so she asked to swap lessons with me. I hope that's okay."

"Sure," I said. "We're picking up on the next chapter of practical magic today, right?"

"We are," she said. "You do still want to start on battle magic, right?"

"Yeah, I do." It'd been my idea to learn how to defend myself using magic, but since I was still a relative newbie, I'd opted to start with some of the simpler spells. Like the freeze-frame spell, specifically to deal with foes who were much faster and stronger than I was.

Since I still had vampires on the brain, it was good timing… or bad, thanks to my restless night of bad dreams involving being caught in a standoff between a bunch of vampires and the Grim Reaper.

I did my best to put it out of mind and pulled out my wand. Estelle raised her own wand, conjuring up a miniature flock of birds which swooped around the room.

"I thought it was easier to practise on a moving target," she explained. "I would have asked Spark or Jet to volunteer, but I'm not sure they'd appreciate being used as target practise. And Sylvester *definitely* wouldn't."

"Nah, it's best if I start out practising on something that isn't real," I said. "Just in case I use the wrong spell."

Unlike biblio-witch magic, casting spells using a wand required a high level of precision and a steady hand, and an attempt at a conjuring charm could easily end up with everyone being turned into squirrels. Even a simple spell like this one had the potential to go dramatically wrong.

"Like this, Rory." Estelle gave another demonstration, halting the birds mid-motion with a perfectly cast freeze-frame spell. "Ready to try?"

I took aim and fired off a freeze-frame spell at the flock of birds. A jet of light escaped my wand and shot right past them, bouncing off the wall.

"Hang on, I'll slow them down." Once again, Estelle aimed her own wand at the flock of miniature birds.

"It doesn't matter," I said. "I need to learn to aim at fast targets."

Like vampires, who moved quickly enough to escape notice unless they deliberately slowed down to an ordinary human level. The image of the vampire I thought I'd seen on the bridge yesterday infiltrated my mind, bringing goose bumps to my arms. Doing my best to push it aside, I waved my wand, and this time, the leading bird froze in mid-flight.

"Nice going," said Estelle. "Try the rest."

I raised my wand again. While half my spells made contact with their targets, each time I missed, my frustration grew. How was I supposed to defend myself against vampires if I couldn't deflect a magical illusion?

I pictured the vampire in my mind, gritted my teeth, and a jet of air shot out of my wand, hitting Estelle instead of the bird.

"Sorry!" I lowered my wand.

Estelle didn't move an inch. Her body had frozen mid-movement, as though I'd hit a pause switch. Naturally, that's when the classroom door opened.

"What's going on here?" Cass wanted to know. "You freeze-framed Estelle? Nice going."

"Battle magic," I responded. "An accident."

"That's not battle magic, that's *I'm running for my life* magic," she said. "Battle magic is when you hit back, not flee for the hills."

"There's some occasions where you're better off running," I told her. "Like if you're being chased by a runaway manticore, for instance."

"You'd better not be thinking of practising on my pets," she said warningly. "Not now you've frozen my sister. You're not still paranoid about vampires, are you?"

I gave her a scowl. She'd more or less stopped teasing me about my fear of vampires, but I maintained that it was a logical fear. The times I'd been cornered by vampires had been among the most terrifying experiences of my life.

Estelle remained frozen. I peered at her. "Is the spell supposed to last that long?"

"No." Sylvester soared overhead and sat on Estelle's head, raking his claws through her hair. "Such a pity. She'll have to stand in the middle of the library as a permanent statue."

"Hilarious." I raised my wand. "Sylvester, get off Estelle's head."

"No, stay there." Cass snickered. "Tell you what, we'll dye her grey, too. I bet Mum won't be able to tell the difference."

Estelle startled back into movement, dislodging the owl, who flew towards me with a screech. On instinct, I fired off the freeze-frame spell and hit Sylvester mid-flight.

"Oh, no." I lowered my wand. "Didn't mean to do that."

Sylvester hovered suspended in mid-air, wings

outstretched, like a stuffed animal hanging from the ceiling.

"At least we know you've got the hang of the spell," said Estelle.

"Do Aunt Candace next," Cass said.

"Cass, stop that." I looked up at Sylvester's frozen body. "He's going to kill me, isn't he?"

"Probably." Cass left the room. "Good luck."

I made to follow her, but Sylvester unfroze in mid-air and spread his wings to catch his balance.

"An outrage!" Sylvester spluttered. "How dare you! May your milk always be off and your bus always late."

I instinctively raised my arms over my head in case he tried clawing me, but he merely flew out the room through the open door, as though he thought I might fire a spell at him again.

"Guess that's his idea of cursing me." My face heated. "Sorry, Estelle."

"Don't worry about it," she said. "Cass turned me into a potted plant during one of our lessons."

"Have you ever hit Sylvester, though?"

She winced. "Well... no."

I'd better hope I didn't need to consult the Forbidden Room at any point soon. Granted, it wouldn't do any good to ask the Book of Questions about the recent death in town. Instead, I needed to wait to hear from Xavier. No matter how much it tried my patience to wait without knowing if his boss had locked him up as punishment for sneaking out of town... or even if the Grim Reaper had barred him from seeing me ever again. He'd almost done so once already, and while he'd given us permission to carry on dating for now, that didn't mean he couldn't abruptly withdraw that permission if he felt like it. If, say, Xavier decided to skip out on his duties by coming with me to visit my best friend.

As long as the Grim Reaper had been the one to deal with the victim's soul and escorted it safely into the afterlife, there was no harm done—but I sincerely hoped he hadn't figured out Xavier and I had deceived him. For all our sakes.

3

My day did not improve in the slightest after my lesson was over. With Sylvester sulking somewhere upstairs, I had to find the most difficult books alone, including a blood-red volume of magical arts which started a fight with two other books on the first floor and forced me to lock them in separate rooms until they calmed down.

It was a great relief when Xavier showed up at lunchtime, and even more so that he'd brought a bag of goodies from Zee's bakery for me.

"Cheers." I took a muffin from the bag and bit into it. "I take it the boss didn't place you under house arrest?"

"Luckily, no," he commented. "But I did find out whose body showed up in the river."

I choked on my mouthful. "Who?"

"The person who died was a vampire," said Xavier. "And he also wasn't a citizen of Ivory Beach."

I swallowed my mouthful of muffin. "So that's why you weren't called to escort his soul into the afterlife?"

As far as I knew, vampires' souls didn't go to the same afterlife as regular human souls after death, because they weren't alive *or* dead in the usual sense. The Grim Reaper rarely delegated vampires' cases to Xavier—he'd mentioned recently to me that he'd never reaped a vampire's soul before—but I'd seen him take down a couple of rogue vamps with relative ease.

Xavier dipped his head. "The Grim Reaper isn't pleased with me for not being around to help him out, but he doesn't know we went as far from town as we did."

He doesn't know. Relief washed over me. Our secret was safe, for now. But Evangeline, for one, wouldn't be pleased to know the body of a vampire had shown up in the river. A vampire who hadn't even been from Ivory Beach.

Wait a second. Evangeline had heard our conversation the previous day. She'd known Xavier and I would be out of town, and the Reaper's apprentice would be unavailable. Which… might mean nothing at all. I shouldn't jump to conclusions, especially where the vampires were concerned. Still…

"Are you working today, then?" I asked.

"Unfortunately," he said. "I just thought I'd drop by to reassure you that we aren't going to be lectured into the afterlife by my boss or barred from ever leaving town again."

"Good." A relieved smile broke out on my face, despite my lingering worries. "I'm glad something's going right. Anyway, do you know who the vampire was? The one who died? I take it he wasn't someone important to Evangeline?"

"I wouldn't know," he said. "Why?"

"Just trying to gauge whether I need to duck the next time she comes to the library." I tensed when the door opened, but it was only a group of students. "I'd better help them out. See you later, okay?"

I carried on helping people find books for the rest of the afternoon, though my mind kept going back to the vampires and Evangeline's strange appearance here the other day. The harder I tried not to think about her, the more she haunted my thoughts.

When my aunt came to the desk to take over from me, I said, "Aunt Adelaide, do you know which books Evangeline was looking for?"

"Why?" she asked.

"Just curious," I said. "She usually at least tries to find one of us when she comes in here." Meaning, me, because she rarely missed an opportunity to play mind games with me.

"Not necessarily," she said. "Evangeline plays by her own rules, I've learned."

"True." The leader of the vampires rarely did anything for no reason, but her mind-reading powers made us mere mortals as transparent to the vampires as they were opaque to us. It was almost impossible to discern their motives, and Evangeline was older and cleverer than most.

I'd seen her walking out of the stacks up on the first floor. Maybe it was a long shot, but I saw no harm in having a look around to see if I could work out which section she'd been in.

I volunteered to take some of the returns up to the first floor, then I headed down the route I'd seen her walking along, reading the labels on the shelves. Magical theory, mostly. Languages—Estelle spent a lot of time in that section these days, learning to understand and communicate with the pixie—and… magical codes. The moment I spotted a box lying on a nearby table, suspicion gripped me.

My aunt's translator spell. It wasn't supposed to be up here.

I picked up the box, carefully, and opened it. Nothing was inside it. Did I really expect Evangeline to have left any clues behind? Had she even been the one to bring it up here? I blamed my trip down memory lane for my paranoia returning in full force. Shaking my head, I finished returning the books to their respective shelves, then went downstairs to find Aunt Adelaide again.

"Did someone leave this upstairs?" I held out the translator spell.

She took it from me. "Perhaps my sister decided to borrow it again."

"It was in the section on magical codes, which was where Evangeline was nosing around," I said. "I wonder if she was trying to give it a test run?"

Aunt Adelaide's gaze shadowed. "Maybe, but I also found her name beside a book she took out of the library a few weeks ago. She was supposed to return it today, but there's been no sign of it."

"Really?" I arched a brow. "I take it she didn't take out one of the books which starts screaming when it's returned late?"

"No, but I'd prefer not to have to send Sylvester to hound her," she said. "I suspect this business with the dead vampire might have distracted her."

"Who was the vampire who died, do you know?" I asked.

"I heard his name was Rudolph Mint," said Aunt Adelaide. "According to Edwin, anyway. He's trying to get the vampires to take the body to bury among their own kind, but since the victim wasn't from town, they don't want to know."

I didn't recognise the name. Nor did I know if he was known to Evangeline or not, though being as old as she was, she knew most of the vampires in the area and others further afield. While I wasn't exactly enthused at the notion of visiting her, at least I now had a reason to show up on her doorstep without drawing her suspicion. Sylvester was usually in charge of late fees, but I doubted he'd agree to be my backup after I'd accidentally frozen him.

"Where is Sylvester?" I asked.

"Sulking," she said. "He said you hit him with a spell."

"It was an accident, believe it or not," I said. "Anyway, do you want me to go and speak to Evangeline? I'll take Jet with me."

Aunt Adelaide's mouth pinched with concern, but she said, "All right. Give me a shout if you need me."

"Jet?" I called, and my familiar swooped down to land on my shoulder. "We're going to see the vampires. That means you have to put on your scary face."

"Yes, partner!" Jet shuffled across my shoulder, gripping my cloak with his clawed feet. The little crow was as far from scary as possible, but at least I felt less alone when I left the library and crossed the square, heading up the high street towards the old church where the vampires spent their days.

Evangeline herself stood outside the church, behind the iron gate, as though she'd expected me to come. Since her ability only extended to reading minds if the person was right in front of her, I figured that she just had a knack for timing. That, or she'd remembered the book she hadn't returned yet.

"Aurora," she said.

"Hey," I said. "Um. Sorry about your friend. If he was your friend, I mean."

Her expression didn't change. "He was not. You were on an excursion outside of town at the time, were you not?"

"I was visiting a friend." It wasn't like going to see my friends in the normal world was a crime, so it was beyond me to figure out what she wanted to achieve by bringing that up. Unless it was a veiled threat to tell tales on Xavier to his boss. "I know you've had a lot going on, but I'm here to ask if you still have the book you borrowed from our library."

"Ah, yes. One second."

She was gone and back in a blink, leaving a blurred impression on my eyelids. *Bloody vampires.* An instant later, her extended hand pushed the book into my palms. Its dark leathery cover was covered in dubious-looking stains.

"Those were already there," she said, reading my thoughts. *Vampires.* Why had I thought coming to see her was a good idea again?

"Go on," she said. "I can sense your curiosity about Rudolph Mint's death. You want my opinion on who killed him."

Heat crept up my neck, but I did my best to keep my

attention fixed on the book, without letting any wayward thoughts of my dad's journal or Xavier or the Grim Reaper flit into view. "I heard he wasn't from Ivory Beach. Did he come from another paranormal town?"

Nobody else seemed to be talking about it either, from what I'd seen. Except for my family, but they'd only been keeping an eye out in case anything caught the Grim Reaper's attention. In other words, if anyone died. Morbid, perhaps, but I had the impression he found nothing worthy of notice except for corpses and his apprentice.

"The vampire who died was a stranger, one who should not have been on my territory," she said. "I did not know he was here. It's a tragedy, really."

Her tone wasn't the slightest bit sincere. Which proved nothing, given that Evangeline cared little for anyone outside of her immediate circle.

"Um, I heard Edwin wanted you to take care of the body," I pressed on. "In the absence of anyone else."

Probably because the odds of a vampire waking up and climbing out of their coffin were considerably higher than a regular corpse. Which wasn't a creepy thought at all.

A smile exposed her sharp teeth. "Yes, that's always a risk. We plan to burn the body to reduce the risk."

"Uh. Good." *I think.* "Haven't they done, uh, an autopsy or anything? To figure out how he died?"

"I suggest you ask Edwin," she said. "I know nothing about this man."

"Okay. Thanks for telling me."

I turned away and left, suppressing the impulse to look

over my shoulder. If she wanted to follow me, she could overtake me in a split second.

Thankfully, though, I reached the library unchallenged. Jet and I entered the lobby, and I let out a relieved breath.

"No trouble?" asked Aunt Adelaide.

"Nope, but Evangeline did her usual mind-reading tricks and tried to creep me out," I said. "She claims nobody in town knows who the guy was or how he ended up in the river. Are there other paranormal towns in the area where he might have come from?"

"There's Elderberry Crescent, which is a few miles north," she said. "I'm sure the police will find out who he was. As for you, Rory, I'd suggest you put it out of mind, if you can. Did you get the book from Evangeline?"

I pulled it out of my bag gingerly. The ominous stains didn't help the impression that the leader of the vampires had something to hide. I'd also forgotten to ask her about the translator spell or what she'd been doing up in the magical codes section, but it might not have been her who'd moved it, and it wasn't worth risking her ire by making accusations.

"Put it in the returns pile." She glanced over her shoulder as the sound of a door slamming open rang through the library. Not the front door, but one of the classrooms at the back of the ground floor.

"Oh no," I said. "I think one of the three books I locked up earlier might have found a way to get out the door."

"I'll deal with it." While she ran across the lobby towards the Reading Corner at the back, I checked the code on the side of the book Evangeline had given me and then picked up the long roll of paper which told me the corresponding section I needed to return it to.

It came as no surprise to learn it had come from the Vampire Section, behind one of the locked doors up on the first floor. A brief check of the book's contents told me it appeared to be written in Latin, which I'd never learned to read. Curiosity pushed aside my unease, and I made for the stairs before I lost my nerve.

Up on the first floor, I found the door to the Vampire Section, its wooden surface painted black and decorated with cobwebs. Real ones or not, who knew. I used my Biblio-Witch Inventory to unlock the door, revealing a gloomy corridor which darkened even further when I stepped inside it.

I scanned the walls for a light switch, but the instant I stepped over the threshold, the door slammed behind me. My heart hammered against my ribcage as though trying to escape my chest.

"Is someone there?" I called out.

Someone like a certain misanthropic owl, for instance? No response came, though I hadn't really expected one.

"All right, then." I fumbled in my pocket for my Biblio-Witch Inventory, but without being able to see the pages, I wouldn't be able to accurately pinpoint the word 'light' without risking accidentally tapping on the wrong word and casting another spell entirely. My wand carried the same risk. One misapplied wave and I might end up transforming myself into a beetle or something. Then I could say goodbye to ever getting out of this room.

Okay. Time for my backup plan. I dug deep into the bottom of my coat pocket and managed to locate my spare notepad and pen. Then I pressed the pen into the page and wrote *light.*

The room remained utterly dark. Maybe I'd used the wrong end of the pen. I flipped it over and tried again, with the same result.

"Oh, come on." The library was playing tricks on me. Or Sylvester, perhaps. Either way, I wouldn't be able to find the right shelf for the book Evangeline had given me, but maybe I could just toss it in here and it'd find its way back where it belonged. You never knew.

I shuffled a few more steps, then dropped the book. At once, light bloomed overhead, enough to illuminate the outline of a shadowy wraithlike creature reaching out a spindly hand for the book.

"Ahh!" I jumped back, tripping over the edge of my cloak and dropping my pen on the floor. The wraith-thing grabbed the book, then hissed at me. I fetched up against the door, finding it still closed. Crouching, I gingerly reached out a hand to retrieve my pen. At once, a tendril of darkness lashed at me, making me recoil.

"I'm not trying to harm you!" I squeaked. "I just wanted out. Um, can I have my pen back?"

The tendrils of shadow engulfed the pen, pulling it into the darkness.

Okay, never mind.

While the creature didn't appear to have any teeth to eat me with, that didn't make me any keener to tempt fate. I had to get out. Fumbling for my wand, I cast an unlocking charm. To my intense relief, the door sprang open this time. Not prepared to take any chances, I slammed the door, re-locked it, and fled for the stairs. I didn't stop sprinting until I reached the lobby, where I collapsed against the front desk.

"Rory!" Estelle gave me an alarmed look. "What's wrong?"

"I just returned a book to the Vampire Section," I said, breathlessly. "Is it supposed to be pitch black in there?"

"The *Vampire* Section?" She crossed the lobby to the front desk. "If you'd let me know, I would have taken it back myself."

"My fault." I sucked in a deep breath. "I got curious about the book Evangeline took out, but the door locked itself behind me. I take it it's not supposed to do that?"

"No." She tutted. "That owl."

"I knew it." I scowled in the direction of the ceiling in case Sylvester was hiding within sight of the lobby.

"He'll get bored soon enough," she said. "Which book did Evangeline take out, then?"

"It was written in Latin and covered in bloodstains," I said. "I assume they were bloodstains, anyway, but she claimed they were already there before she got her hands on the book."

"Bloodstains?" Estelle pulled a face. "Vampires do like playing up to stereotypes."

"Speaking of which, what was with the monster hiding in the shelves?" I asked. "It grabbed the book off me and ran off with it."

"Oh, a book-wraith," she said. "They're fairly harmless creatures that feed on the power inside our ancient titles. They really like books written in Latin, for some reason."

"That would explain why it was so keen to get the book off me." I heaved a shudder. "It also stole my pen."

"I'll get you another one," she said. "And next time you

have to return a book up there, tell me first and I'll handle it."

"Nah, I have to get used to dealing with the nightmares section eventually."

"You joke, but there actually is a nightmares section," she said. "Don't worry, you won't get to that one for a while, though."

"I'm not setting foot near anything dangerous as long as Sylvester insists on nursing a grudge," I told her.

At this rate, I might be better served learning to defend myself against owls instead of vampires.

4

The following day, I woke to an abominable shrieking noise. Sylvester sat on my bed post, singing what sounded like a butchered version of a Taylor Swift song.

"Stop that!" I shooed him away. "You nearly got me eaten alive by a shadowy monster yesterday. Haven't you tormented me enough?"

"Certainly not," he hooted. "What would be the fun of you getting eaten alive if it meant you'd no longer be here for me to torment?"

I grabbed a handful of glitter the pixie had dropped on my bedside table and waved it threateningly until he flew out of the room. Then I checked my phone to find a message from Laney: *when can I visit?*

Now's not a great time, I wanted to reply. For a multitude of reasons, none of which I could mention in a text message. She'd think I'd been reading too many horror novels if I started going on about dead vampires and creepy shadow-monsters and diabolical owls.

I dressed and got ready for the day while pondering on how to reply, and then went downstairs to find all my family members sitting around the kitchen table. Given Cass's antisocial tendencies and Aunt Candace's penchant for being wrapped up in her own little world, this was a rare occurrence.

"Ah, Rory," said Aunt Adelaide. "I saved you some breakfast before Candace ate it all."

"Thanks," I said, gratefully pulling the one free plate towards me. "Is there any reason we're all gathered in here?"

"Your aunt has an interview."

"Oh?" I turned to Aunt Candace. "Not a job interview?"

I was under the impression she made a decent enough living from her books—and besides, there was always the library, even if the job of running the place mostly fell to Aunt Adelaide and Estelle.

"No, of course not," said Aunt Candace. "I'm the one doing the interview. It's for research. I'm writing a prison break novel."

I gave an eye-roll. "Please tell me you're not going to pester poor Edwin again."

"Not at all," she said. "I'm going north to visit Elderberry Crescent."

Isn't that where the vampire might have come from? "Why go there when we have a jail right here in Ivory Beach? Not that I'm encouraging you to start badgering Edwin, but I thought you'd want to stay closer to home."

Aunt Candace often went weeks without leaving the library at all, let alone visiting another town.

"Yes, but there's a first time for everything," she said.

Uh-huh. I had an inkling there must be more to it than that. There usually was.

I took a bite of toast, but my appetite fled when Aunt Candace turned to hiss at her sister, "No, I'm not looking for a vampire."

"What was that about vampires?" I put my toast back on my plate. "*Did* the victim come from Elderberry Crescent?"

"He did," Aunt Adelaide said. "Granted, he doesn't seem to have been very popular. Nobody from the town came to check on him after his disappearance."

"As for *why* he's so unpopular?" Aunt Candace said, her eyes alight with mischief. "It seems he was a member of a certain sect of vampires known among the initiated as the Founders. A group whose sole mission is to hunt for knowledge and secrets."

My throat went dry. Was the victim part of the same group as Mortimer Vale and the other two vampires who'd been after my dad's journal?

"He was?" I asked. "You didn't happen to find out how he died?"

"Staked," said Aunt Candace. "Unimaginative, if you ask me."

"Staked," I repeated. "A human killed him?"

"Not necessarily," said Estelle. "If anything, vampires are more likely to have the speed and strength necessary to stake another of their kind. They're hard for humans to kill."

Didn't I know it. There'd been a case a few months ago where someone had stolen the Grim Reaper's scythe and used it to slaughter vampires, but that was a rare exception to the rule.

"Maybe, but that doesn't mean a human didn't manage it," said Aunt Candace. "It's always who you least expect."

Cass made a sceptical noise. "Whoever did it, do you expect us to ignore that the vampire in question was on the run from jail when he died?"

"You mean the same jail where you're conducting an interview today?" I raised an eyebrow at Aunt Candace. "You expect me to buy this *researching a novel* excuse?"

"Everything can be research for a novel," she insisted. "Even the death of a mysterious undead prisoner in even more mysterious circumstances."

She rose to her feet, her pen and notebook floating alongside her, and walked out of the kitchen.

Estelle shook her head. "I tried talking to her."

"So did I," said Aunt Adelaide.

"I didn't bother," Cass put in. "There's no stopping her when she's on a mission."

"Aren't you a little concerned that she might bring the vampire's killer back into town?" I said. "It's one thing when she researches brutal crimes from decades in the past, but we're talking about a murder which happened this week. And the killer might still be in the area, for all we know."

Maybe even in the town itself. Like Mortimer Vale. He'd been locked in jail ever since he'd tried to kill me upon my arrival in town, but that didn't mean he wasn't up to date on the latest news from the region. Not to mention I'd thought I'd seen one of his companions on the bridge back home. If the murder victim had been part of the same group of vampires who'd chased me out of town, it was harder to pass off the incident as a product of my overactive imagination.

"Who cares?" said Cass. "The murder is none of our business."

"The victim was probably known to Mortimer Vale," I told Cass. "That makes it our business, on account of the fact that the guy kind of tried to murder me. Twice."

"And he's in jail, so that makes it irrelevant," she said. "I thought you'd stopped with this nonsense by now."

"It's not nonsense if someone died for it," Estelle reprimanded. "Look, the Founders' primary goal is to seek out knowledge, and what's the biggest centre of magical knowledge in the region? The library. I don't *think* they'll target Aunt Candace for nosing around and conducting interviews, but we should at least keep an eye on the situation."

"The Founders have never targeted the library before." Cass rose to her feet. "Let Aunt Candace go on a research spree, by all means, but don't drag our family into any more vampire drama."

And with that, Cass left the kitchen, shaking her head.

"They *have* been here before," I pointed out, but she didn't turn back. "They came after my dad's journal. Has she forgotten?"

"Unlikely," said Estelle. "She just has issues with the idea of anyone threatening the library."

"If Candace brings any threats after her, the library will deal with them," said Aunt Adelaide.

"Speaking of which, when will I learn to control the library the way you guys can?" I asked. "I know it's a long shot, but Laney still has her heart set on meeting all of you and seeing the library. There must be a way to make it safe for normals, right?"

"The issue, Rory, is that all of us would need to agree

to hide our magic at the same time," said Aunt Adelaide. "That means humans *and* familiars."

"Of course that includes Sylvester." I rolled my eyes. "I guess I'll have to convince him to forgive me if I want to invite my best friend here without him locking us both in the same room as a sinister pen-stealing book wraith."

Aunt Adelaide pressed her mouth together. "Are there any balloons left?"

"No, unfortunately." Sylvester had had endless fun bursting the balloons we'd found in an abandoned upstairs corridor and repurposed for Valentine's Day, but I didn't have anything similar in reserve to tempt him with.

"I'll have a word with him." She left the kitchen, while I finished up breakfast and helped Estelle clear away the dishes.

While Estelle headed into the stacks to deal with the day's returns, I called my familiar. "Jet, can you go to the town's jail and see if you hear Mortimer's name mentioned? Or the murdered vampire?"

"Of course, partner!" He took off in a beat of his wings, while I busied myself with the tasks of the day and tried to put Aunt Candace's quest for information out of mind.

I began to regret sending Jet away when Sylvester volunteered to fetch a book for me and then 'accidentally' dropped it on my head.

"Ow!" I crouched down and retrieved the large hardback, stars winking before my eyes. "That's not even from the right section. I didn't ask for a treatise on water plants."

Sylvester swooped down and grabbed the book in his beak, knocking me onto my rear. I got to my feet, only to be bowled over again when the owl came hooting back with two other irrelevant titles in his beak. I scrambled backwards, not fast enough to avoid both books hitting me on the head at the same time.

"If you've given me a concussion, I'll make you take over the desk in my place." I rubbed my forehead.

"If you think I'll leave you alone if you're stuck in a hospital bed, you're mistaken." He flew away, cackling to himself.

I was starting to wish I'd accompanied Aunt Candace as her assistant while she interviewed people at Elderberry Crescent's jail. Which was saying a lot, because in normal circumstances, I'd want to be as far away as possible from her when she was on one of her research missions. Like the other side of the planet, for instance.

"Sylvester!" Estelle came to my rescue, with the pixie in tow. "Stop tormenting Rory."

"I said I was sorry for freezing you," I added to the owl, who ignored me. "You're going to have to get over it at some point."

"Oh, you don't think I can hold a long-term grudge, do you?" Sylvester said.

"I assumed you were more mature than that," I said pointedly, but the owl ignored me and swooped off, nearly colliding with the pixie going in the opposite direction. "Maybe I need a bodyguard."

Estelle and I retrieved the right book for the patron waiting behind the desk, who probably thought we were all a few cards short of a deck. The clamour of the owl and the pixie fighting sent Estelle running for the stairs, so I stepped in to deal with the next visitor.

"Hey," I said. "Can I help you?"

A red-haired young man approached the desk. "Yes, I'm looking for *Military Magic: Volume Twenty-Five.*"

"Sure, that's on the ground floor," I said, pleased to find I remembered without having to look it up. "I'll just get that for you."

I slipped out from behind the counter and made my way through the stacks to a section near the back of the reference area. While I'd had no trouble remembering its location, I'd never actually been there before. Confusingly, all the titles in that section had the same metallic grey covers, while two identical shelves faced one another on either side of me, each containing the same volumes in the same order. *That's weird.*

I read the spines before reaching for the correct volume from the shelf on my right, then startled when both shelves moved at the same time, folding in on themselves until the books were on the inside and not the outside. With a rumbling noise, mechanical arms rose from each side until two swords and two shields faced one another.

"Hang on!" I stood between them. "What are you doing? I just need a volume of magical military history. Not a duel."

The shelves ignored me. Whereabouts the books had disappeared to, I had no idea, but I hoped they'd be safe from any damage. One of the shelves swung a sword at the other, which parried with a metallic grating sound which was probably audible up on the top floor.

"Stop that!" I grabbed for my Biblio-Witch Inventory and jabbed the word *halt*, but it didn't work. So much for this being an easy job.

I went for my wand instead, casting the freeze-frame

spell. To my intense relief, the shelves froze mid-motion, swords crossed with one another.

"Rory!" Estelle ran into view, the pixie on her shoulder. "What's going on?"

I gestured at the frozen shelves. "I get that it's the Military Magic section, but it's not much use if I can't actually get any of the books off the shelves."

"Oh, I know what the problem is," she said. "You have to take a copy of the book you need from both shelves at the same time. If you take from one and not the other, they start duelling."

"Good to know." I watched, bemused, as she walked between the duelling shelves and waved her wand. At once, the swords and shields disappeared, and the shelves reverted back to their normal appearance. "So I have to take out two copies of the book?"

"You've got it." She stepped aside to let me through, while I scanned the shelves for the volume I needed. Then I did the same on the opposite side before reaching for both shelves at once, pulling a book off each of them. I tensed, waiting for swords and shields to appear again, but the shelves shifted in a satisfied rustle of pages.

"Now I've seen it all." I carried both books through to the front desk, filing the new information into the back of my mind. Part of being a biblio-witch was learning to navigate each section of the library's specific quirks, so I'd probably still be learning when I'd been here a decade. Still, it was an improvement on the incident with the Vampire Section.

I handed one copy of the book to the student while Estelle put the spare volume on the desk.

"Is Sylvester behaving?" I asked her.

"I sent him up to bother Cass instead," she said. "Which he won't, because she's his favourite person."

"I'm probably his least favourite at this point," I remarked. "Is the pixie okay?"

The little pixie zipped around my head, making chittering noises.

"He says he's fine," said Estelle. "It'll take more than an angry owl to frighten him off."

"The language lessons are going well, then?" None of us spoke the pixie's language, but Estelle had taken it upon herself to learn from scratch after adopting him as her new assistant.

"You bet." Estelle held out a hand and the pixie landed on her wrist, his little wings beating. "Where's Jet?"

"I sent him to snoop around the jail and see if Mortimer Vale is up to no good," I admitted. "Just in case someone else attempts a breakout. Or Aunt Candace shows up."

"Oh, so that's why you had to get Sylvester's help and not Jet's." She turned to the pixie, and he made a chattering noise in response. "He says he'll help you until Jet comes back."

"Thanks." I smiled at her. "I doubt he'll be long. It's not like he's going as far as Aunt Candace is."

Sure enough, Jet returned within several minutes, flying through the library with his little wings pumping.

"Any news?" I asked. "Was Mortimer Vale acting suspiciously at all?"

"No, partner!" he said. "The prisoner is being well-behaved, the elf says. He's ignoring everyone."

"Did he ask about Rudolph Mint's death?" I asked.

"No, partner, but I heard two of the trolls discussing the case. They decided to increase security."

"In case anyone gets any ideas from his escape," I surmised. "Thanks, Jet."

I'd wait and see what Aunt Candace said before jumping to any conclusions, but it didn't sound like Mortimer Vale was involved in any of the group's activities now he was behind bars. Then again, that didn't mean he held no influence over the others, nor that he wasn't paying any attention to the case. The vampire who'd died had been a member of the Founders, after all.

I was glad Edwin was taking the potential security threat seriously, at least, but was the victim a friend or foe of Mortimer Vale's? And who, exactly, had killed him?

Not long after the library closed for the day, Aunt Candace returned, her cheeks flushed from the cold and her hair wilder than ever. "Well, that was enlightening."

"In what way?" I looked for the others, but Aunt Adelaide had gone to make dinner while Estelle returned the military books to their respective shelves. Only Jet and I remained in the lobby. "You didn't get kicked out for asking questions, did you? Or get us put on a watchlist?"

"Hardly," she said. "You can get away with asking anything if it's for research."

"I think that depends on who you're asking," I said pointedly, not forgetting the time Xavier had come for dinner with my family and she'd decided to interrogate him about the Grim Reaper's closely guarded secrets. Not to mention she'd traumatised poor Edwin the one time he'd held her overnight in a cell.

Aunt Candace, who seemed to have forgotten both incidents, said, "Well, the nice man at the prison was very keen to talk to me. I have enough material for a series, in fact."

"Just as long as you don't try acting out the prison break," I said. "Did he seem keen to talk about the vampire who escaped, then?"

"I wouldn't say *keen,* but he did tell me that this Rudolph Mint was known to our delightful friend who currently resides in our own jail."

Mortimer Vale. I knew it. "Friend or enemy?"

"I don't know," she said. "With the vampires, it's rather tricky to tell, and the prison staff were fairly traumatised by his abrupt escape. He knocked two of them out."

"Ugh." I shivered. "So Mortimer knew the victim. They were both part of the same little clique. Did you ask about the circumstances of Rudolph Mint's death?"

"Of course I did," said Aunt Candace. "Turns out the local vampires had a big fancy party at a manor house near Elderberry Crescent, around the same time as he broke out of jail."

Chills raced down my spine. "A party? To celebrate what?"

"Do the vampires need an excuse for a party?" she queried. "I got the impression it was more of a meeting held by members of the Founders in order to exchange secrets."

"Does Evangeline know?" I asked.

"I wouldn't know," she said. "I doubt she'll be trekking all the way over to Elderberry Crescent to ask. What does it matter to her if a vampire outsider dies on her territory?"

I pressed my mouth together. It did matter. Especially for those of us who'd made enemies of the Founders. But with nobody else to ask, the only person in town who might have the answers was Mortimer Vale himself.

5

Edwin considered me. "You want to visit *who?*"

"Mortimer Vale." I faced the elf policeman across the desk in the reception area of the local police station. "I think there's a possibility that he might know who killed the vampire who died the other day."

"That's a serious accusation to make without proof," he said. "Even if it was true, Vale has been in here for months."

"I know he has." I swallowed my unease. "The group of vampires he used to work with was in the area the night Rudolph Mint escaped from jail. I know for a fact two of them have been watching my family's library since I moved here."

"Neither of those other vampires has ever been seen near Ivory Beach," said Edwin. "Look, I can appreciate that your family is in a position of vulnerability when it comes to these vampires, but I can't just let you walk in and talk to my prisoners."

"Then why not question him yourself?" I asked. "I'm

assuming the police in Elderberry Crescent would want to know if someone from here might know how one of their prisoners died after escaping custody."

"How on earth did you know that?" Then he tutted. "Your aunt. Please don't tell me she's intending to come here and bother me again."

"She did promise she wouldn't come here," I reassured him. "But she's concerned for the library, as we all are. We don't know anything about Rudolph Mint, but it might be that Mortimer Vale has an idea of who might have been responsible for his death. They belonged to the same group. The Founders."

The elf policeman frowned. "I shouldn't even consider granting your request, but oddly enough, Mortimer Vale was asking after you today."

My heart lurched. "He… he was? What was he asking?"

"He asked if you were still living here in Ivory Beach."

I blinked. "Why would he ask that? It's fairly obvious I am."

"Not to someone who's behind bars," he said.

"He can read minds, though," I said. "There's no way he doesn't know everything that's happened in town since he was locked up, either."

This was just some weird mind game of his, that was all.

The elf clucked his tongue. "Right. I'll have security bring him into an interrogation room, and we'll ask him a few pointed questions. After that, you'll leave. No arguments."

I nodded, apprehension building as I waited in the reception area for the security trolls to bring Mortimer

Vale out of his cell and into one of the interrogation rooms.

My worries doubled with each second that passed, but I couldn't think of another way to get any information on the Founders' movements in the area. If I wanted to prepare for the possibility that the Founders might target the library, I'd have to face the man who'd given me my terrifying induction to the magical world.

One of the trolls gave me a wave, indicating for me to come through the metal door to the interrogation room. Drawing in a breath, I walked into the small room, which contained nothing more than a table and three chairs. Edwin sat in one of them with two trolls standing at his back, and he indicated for me to take the seat on his right.

In the other seat, Mortimer Vale looked me over, his hands cuffed on the table in front of him.

"I did wonder if you were ever going to come and talk to me, Aurora," he said. "I thought your fear would hold you back for the rest of your life."

"Guess you were wrong." My heart gave a thud against my ribcage. "Why were you asking about me? I didn't know you missed me that much."

Alarm bells rang in the back of my mind, especially when his gaze turned probing. I focused all my attention on the edge of the table and refused to let any wayward thoughts seep through.

He tilted his head. "You're less transparent than you were when we first met."

It was nice to know my lessons in learning how to resist vampire mind-reading were having some effect. Didn't mean I trusted him an inch, though.

Edwin leant forward in his seat. "If I perceive you to

be threatening Aurora, then you'll be back behind bars with no further visitors."

"I cannot harm her as long as I am defenceless." He lifted his cuffed hands, which must be made of something designed to hold vampires. They were far stronger than humans, and I'd seen how fast and fluidly they moved when free. A shiver raced up my spine. "Go on, Aurora. Ask your questions."

I drew in a breath. "I suppose you heard that a vampire who belonged to the Founders showed up dead near Ivory Beach the other day?"

"You have interesting ideas about how much information reaches me here in this isolated hellhole, Aurora."

"You can read minds," I pointed out. "I know you need to make eye contact to do it, but it's not like nobody ever comes into the jail to check up on you."

And give him fresh blood, I assumed, considering he didn't look diminished in the slightest after his long imprisonment.

"You've learned a lot about my kind in a short space of time," he said. "I suppose Evangeline will have told you. I expected the two of you would establish a rapport."

"You expected me to become friends with her?" I said incredulously.

"No, but I assumed you'd desire to educate yourself," he said. "And poor Dominic... I heard of his tragic fate. I've long suspected his closeness with humans would be the end of him."

"I didn't know you knew him," I said.

"I know a great many vampires, Aurora. I've been alive for a very long time."

"I gathered," I said. "I assume Rudolph Mint was

among them. Did you know he escaped prison the night of his death, and that there was a gathering of members of the Founders nearby?"

"I wouldn't know," he said. "I did not receive an invitation. It seems I'm not privy to the Founders' concerns."

That was definitely a lie. Not that I could call him out on it without risking him clamming up altogether. How was I supposed to get him to tell the truth when he was the mind-reader and I wasn't?

He gave me a fanged smile. "I have not set foot outside this jail since my imprisonment began, Aurora."

Great. It seemed I was easy to read even when I was doing my level best to keep him from seeing my thoughts. "Then who might have killed him? Anyone from Ivory Beach?"

"I have yet to be acquainted with everyone in this delightful town, because I was incarcerated shortly after my arrival," he said. "I'd advise you to speak to the local vampires yourself."

"You mean, Evangeline?" I tried to read his face, but it was like trying to read that bloodstained tome written in Latin. "You think she'd take kindly to me asking her if she murdered anyone?"

Edwin cleared his throat. "If you're making an accusation, then I'll have to bring Evangeline in myself."

Mortimer Vale barely spared the elf policeman a glance. "That won't be necessary. Evangeline is a strict rule-follower... though she does like collecting knowledge in her own way. Do you hear something outside?"

A faint squeaking noise reached my ears. "What is that?"

"The jail has a rather large rat problem," Mortimer Vale informed Edwin. "I suppose it amuses you to let us live among vermin, but I find them quite agreeable creatures."

"What have you done?" Edwin rose to his feet, calling to his troll guard. "I'll be back, Rory—call for me if you need me."

Then he left the room, leaving me alone with the vampire. And the trolls, though their attention was on the door, and the rising squeaks from the corridor.

Mortimer Vale and I looked at one another for a moment.

"Did you do that, by any chance?" I said. "Rats? Really?"

"Vampires often have an affinity with small rodents," he said. "Aren't you going to thank me?"

"Why would I do that?"

"You wanted to talk to me alone." His smile was back. "I know you're reluctant to ask certain questions in front of your elf friend, particularly ones that implicate the local vampires."

He was right. Unfortunately. "You mean Evangeline? Does she have any connections with the Founders?"

It was a question I'd always been curious to know the answer to. I mean, she'd shown an excessive interest in my dad's journal from the moment she'd learned I had it, but without knowing what information it actually contained, it was impossible for me to figure out if its contents pertained to the Founders alone, or vampires in general.

"Go on," he said. "Ask me what's in the journal. I know you want to. Your curiosity... it's palpable."

I folded my arms across my chest. "And you'll tell me for free? I don't think so."

"Your family have tried to find the solution to the code ever since you brought it to them, haven't they?" he said. "But they have yet to succeed."

I remained silent. As long as I didn't let anything slip, he could only guess at what I knew.

"Such a waste," he said softly. "If I'd been allowed to take the journal, my companions and I would have made much better use of it. Truly, it is wasted on your family."

"It's not yours," I told him.

"Ah, but it concerns my kind rather more than it does yours," he said. "I suppose your father wouldn't have told you… he let you stumble around in total ignorance of the magical world, much less his own shameful past."

What is he talking about?

A cruel smile tugged at his mouth. I didn't need to speak aloud to know my expression was utterly transparent. How could it not be after what he'd just implied?

"You're lying," I said. "My dad wanted to protect me from evil fiends like you. That's why he didn't tell me about the magical world."

"If you're so certain, then why not research the Founders for yourself rather than avoiding them?"

"I'm asking you right now," I said. "I'm not avoiding you."

"Until now, you have been," he said softly. "And if not for this recent death, you still would."

"You don't know what I would or wouldn't do." I stifled the anger brewing inside me, with difficulty. "I'm not convinced *you* know what's in the journal, either.

You're avoiding the subject by playing mind games with me instead of getting to the point."

"If you knew half of what that journal contained, you would never think of your father the same way again," he said. "But you're right in thinking that information comes with a price. I will tell you the truth, if you will unlock these chains and set me free."

"You have got to be kidding me," I said. "You nearly killed me the last time you walked free."

"If you'd given me the journal, then I wouldn't have needed to threaten you or your family."

My hands clenched. "The journal was my dad's. He'd never have wanted me to hand it over to a stranger who threatened my life. Besides, I don't see how it's relevant to this death, aside from the link to the Founders."

"It's relevant because if a Founder was murdered, the others will be looking for the culprit," he said. "It may be that they will gravitate towards a certain repository of knowledge which happens to reside in the vicinity of the individual's death."

The library. Never mind the journal—the library contained countless texts heaving with information the vampires would kill to possess.

"You mean they're coming here?" I swallowed against my dry throat. "Now?"

"I wouldn't know," he said. "I generally learn of events after they happen... like Rudolph Mint's imprisonment and subsequent death."

A chill raced through the room as though from an open window. I became aware of my fast heartbeat and quickening breath as the air around the vampire seemed to tighten. A rare hint of emotion entered his eyes. Not sorrow, but breath-taking rage. The vampire was furious about Rudolph Mint's death. Or his escape, maybe. After all, his jailbreak had led to Mortimer's own security being upped so he had even less chance of breaking out than he had previously. Unless he truly thought I'd willingly unlock his chains in the hopes of learning what he knew.

"I thought we were here to talk about Evangeline, and whether she was connected to the murder or not." I glanced behind me as the sound of footsteps came from the corridor. "Please, just tell me. It's not like it matters to you either way."

"Evangeline is very old," he said. "Like most of us, she has long since grown bored of most games humans play… but the game of knowledge is one that can sustain us for an eternity."

"What does that mean?"

The door opened and Edwin walked in, wearing an aggrieved expression. "Blasted rodents. Are you done, Rory?"

I turned to the vampire, whose expression had shuttered. I had an inkling I wouldn't get any more information out of him, and what he'd told me was alarming enough already.

The murder victim had been Mortimer Vale's friend. A fact that made him angry… and perhaps the other Founders felt the same way.

"Yes." I stood. "I'm done."

I felt the vampire's cold stare on my back as I left the room, but I resisted the impulse to turn back and demand an explanation. His price was too high. Besides, I might not have any leverage to use against him, but that didn't mean I had to take every word he said at face value, either.

Especially what he'd said about my dad and his journal. *That* sounded like a lie constructed to mess with my head. The journal's contents were unknown—even to the vampires, for all I knew—and their desire to possess it didn't mean they could read its contents.

Estelle waited for me outside the door, wearing a concerned expression on her face. "Everything okay?"

I drew in a deep breath. "Mortimer thinks the Founders might be coming here. To the library."

I explained everything I'd inferred from our conversation… and I'd had to infer more than he'd actually given away. By the time we reached the library, Aunt Adelaide had joined us, and I ended up repeating the whole thing a third time when we went into the living room to find Aunt Candace perched on a seat with her notebook and pen hovering at her side, while Cass sat in an armchair with her nose in a book.

"Great," Cass said, when I'd finished explaining. "You'll need that magical combat training, then, if that Mortimer Vale brings all his mates here to pillage our library. Why couldn't you have left it alone?"

"He only told us what we already suspected," Estelle said. "Considering Rudolph Mint died right outside Ivory Beach, they'd have come here whether Rory spoke to Mortimer Vale or not. Did he say anything else?"

"He's *angry* his friend died," I said. "I could tell by his body language. If he's mad, it's not a stretch to say the other vampires in their little clique aren't, too."

"Wonderful," said Cass. "I'll get my manticore ready for guard duty."

"We won't let them get into the library," said Aunt

Adelaide. "We have more than enough defences in place to keep a band of rogues like them from hurting us."

I hoped she was right. Until we knew which other vampires might be involved, all we could do was wait and see.

"Candace?" Aunt Adelaide added to her sister. "You won't let any vampires into the library, will you?"

"Of course not." She looked up from her notebook, a wounded expression on her face. "Wouldn't dream of it."

"He hinted that Evangeline isn't the killer, but who knows whether the facts back it up," I added. "I don't think she's a member of the Founders, but that doesn't mean she might not be after the same target."

And she'd made it quite clear that she looked out for herself alone.

"Meaning the journal," said Cass. "Personally, I'd get a fishing line and dangle that journal over the ocean until they dive in and drown. Problem solved."

"Honestly, Cass." I shook my head. "The journal's on their list, but it's not the only thing they're looking for. Besides, it's not like I know what's in it."

Aunt Adelaide pursed her lips. "I'm going to resume work on the translator spell. I'm sorry for neglecting it, Rory."

"Don't worry about it," I said. "For all I know, the vampires can't read it either and just want to stick it in a cabinet or something. Or sell it for a fortune. Human collectors buy all kinds of weird things, and I'm sure vampire collectors are no different."

Except for one slight issue… his comments about my dad being ashamed of his past, ashamed enough that he'd kept secrets he'd never wanted me to learn. Secrets he'd written in an unreadable code.

Whatever the case, I had a more pressing matter at hand. If we didn't at least try to figure out who'd staked and killed Rudolph Mint, then his friends might well gravitate to the area. Then it would only take one slip for them to learn the Founders had targeted me already. And if they all came after the library, it was more than my neck on the line.

6

I stood on the threshold of the Vampires Section of the library and tried to quell my nerves. With Sylvester still sulking and refusing to let me into the Forbidden Room, I'd taken my mission to learn how to defend myself against vampires into my own hands.

Of course, first I had to get my hands on one of the books without encountering the shadowy book wraith. I'd learned my lesson from last time and cast a spell on the door to keep it open, so I'd have at least one light source to see by. This time, the room wasn't full dark when I shuffled inside. Without the darkness, it wasn't that big, either, a short corridor lined with shelves. No sign of any book wraiths, either. So far, so good.

I scanned the titles on the shelf on my left first, looking for a guide to defending oneself against the vampires in a realistic way. Other than running for my life, that is. While I'd normally take the latter option, the library came with one major downside: it was open to the public, which made it an exception to the usual rule where vampires had to be invited into an establishment in order to enter. No matter what defences my family had at our disposal, we couldn't close that loophole without shutting down the library altogether. Which was why I hoped I'd find a realistic guide on how a human might best a vampire without anyone ending up dead. Or *un*dead.

My regular magical defence textbook hadn't been much help on that front. Magical shields which deflected spells wouldn't do a thing against vampires. Light momentarily dazzled them, but that would barely work as a diversion. Even here in the vampires' own section of the library, the first book I found simply said, *If attacked by a vampire, use a stake or else lie down and accept death.*

I rolled my eyes at the book. "Really helpful."

Using a stake was one of few ways to instantly kill a vampire, but even if the vamp in question *was* a hostile outsider, Evangeline wouldn't appreciate me stabbing any of her fellow undead.

I pushed the book back into place and moved onto the second row of shelves, catching sight of a number of titles similar to the leather-bound volume Evangeline had checked out. Most of them bore suspicious-looking stains, and when I opened one of them, a pair of sharpened fangs snapped at my fingers. I hastily shoved the book back into place before the chattering teeth drew the attention of the book wraith again. Who in their right mind wanted a book with its own set of vampire teeth?

My hand lingered over a volume titled *How to Negotiate with the Undead.* Negotiating with vampires would be a useful skill to have, but a quick scan of the contents confirmed the author didn't have much more of an idea than I did about how the vampires' minds worked. Not being able to read their thoughts meant the vampires were the only authorities on the subject of their kind, and the odds of them making that information available to the general public seemed unlikely. They liked having the upper hand too much to give up their secrets easily.

Mortimer Vale, though? Even if he'd been unaware of the Founders' presence in the area, he must at least know the identities of the possible culprits who might have their sights set on the library. But would one book really give me enough of an edge to convince him to give me answers?

A creaking noise came from behind me. Then darkness fell overhead, masking the shelves.

"Not again." I scrambled for my Biblio-Witch Inventory. After my last disastrous trip in here, I'd done my best to memorise which order the words in my Inventory were in, so I wouldn't need to be able to see the page to find what I needed.

I ran my finger down the list and jabbed it with a finger. Light burst from the pages, temporarily dazzling my eyes as it dispelled the darkness. I backed up from the shelf, lowering the book, and slammed into a solid figure.

With a yelp, I wheeled around to find my chest pressed against Xavier's. I sprang back with a relieved gasp.

"Oh, hey, Rory," said the Reaper. "Sorry, I think I frightened the library into turning off the lights when I walked in here."

"Xavier." I pressed a hand to my thumping heart. "You just scared me half to death."

"Sorry." His gaze went to the shelf in front of me. "You're looking for books on vampires?"

"Yep. Facing my fears and all that."

"I thought the vampire's murder was an isolated incident," he said. "And the victim didn't come from Ivory Beach."

Ah. I hadn't told him about my meeting with Mortimer Vale yet… mostly because my phone hadn't been working last night and I'd needed time to process what the vampire had told me.

"Turns out the guy who died was Mortimer Vale's friend or acquaintance," I began. "And there was a gathering of the Founders in the area the night of his death. They might still be around. You can never be too careful."

"How did you know…?" He broke off. "What is that?"

Shadowy claws reached out from behind the shelf, and a pair of eyes blinked balefully from the gloom.

"I think the room's guardian thinks you're a threat," I commented. "We're not threatening anyone. I'm just looking for a guide to vampiric defence. I know there's supposed to be one in here—"

The book wraith scuttled into view, hissing at both of us. Xavier caught my shoulder and pulled me towards the door.

"Hey!" I braced myself in the doorway. "We're not threatening you. I work here."

A book flew into the air, hitting me full in the face. Xavier caught it before it could fall to the ground, while I slammed the door shut, breathing hard.

"Ow." I rubbed my nose, taking the book from Xavier with my free hand. "What was that in aid of?"

"The library felt threatened," said Cass from behind me. "Did you walk in there and start talking about thieves? No wonder you brought out the book wraith."

"I mentioned Mortimer Vale's name," I admitted, "but I've been walking around the library talking about him for ages without anything like that happening."

"High security areas are a different matter." She rolled her eyes. "You didn't think we had no way to tell if someone was a threat?"

At least we knew the security was working. Assuming it hadn't just been Sylvester messing with me again. "Well, Xavier isn't a threat, and I doubt the Grim Reaper would appreciate it if his apprentice got locked in an upstairs corridor with a cranky monster on the loose."

"Speaking of whom, I should probably head back." Xavier made for the stairs, and I fell into step alongside him. "He's been in one of his paranoid moods ever since the vampire's death. Is that the book you were looking for?"

"I hope so, because we just ticked off its guardian." I checked the title of the book the wraith had thrown at me. *Vampire Defence,* it was called. That seemed promising. "It's the best I could do, since Sylvester isn't speaking to me and Jet hasn't got to that section yet."

"Why isn't Sylvester speaking to you?" asked Xavier.

"I accidentally froze him in the middle of a magic lesson," I said. "In my defence, he was flying around being annoying."

"I can see that," said Xavier. "Don't let the vamps get you down, okay? Tell you what, we should go out for a meal tomorrow after your shift. That sound good?"

"Sure." I hugged him goodbye, then went to join Estelle at the front desk. "Need help with those returns?"

"I thought you were practising magic," she said.

"I got chased out the Vampire Section again," I said. "I

was looking for advanced combat books for magical defence against vampires."

"There's no need to look in the advanced section," she said. "Tell you what, I'll give you a lesson myself. My mum can take over at the desk. I'll just take this last return back and I'll join you in a second."

"Sure." I gave her a smile. "I appreciate it."

I headed into an empty classroom and opened the book I'd grabbed earlier, turning to Chapter One. The header said, *How to Use Speed and Strength to Overcome Your Prey*. Well, that didn't sound particularly helpful.

I flicked through the pages, pausing at an illustration of two vampires biting a defenceless human. *Ugh. Not what I needed to see.*

In fact, it seemed the book wraith had had the last laugh and thrown a book at me which was designed to instruct vampires on how to defend *themselves*. As if they needed any more advantages.

"Seriously?" I turned the pages, grimacing at each new chapter title. When I reached the chapter titled *Taking Care of Your Human,* which featured in-depth instructions for finding and convincing a human to turn into a willing subjugate, I gave up reading and started skimming.

Near the back, I finally found what I was looking for in the form of a brief chapter on *Defending Yourself Against Specific Weaknesses.* Even then, the author spent three pages waxing poetic on the vampires' superiority to every other living species in the magical world.

"Get on with it, already," I muttered, skipping through the chapter.

On the very last page, I found a brief list: *Avoid fire and running water.*

That was it for weaknesses, it seemed. I'd already known vampires hated fire. They also couldn't cross running water, but the rules on what counted as running water were complicated, so fire was my best bet. There must be a fire-conjuring spell, right? Admittedly, the library might not be the best place to practise that one.

In my pocket, my phone buzzed. Another message from Laney: *"I found Ivory Beach."*

I stared at the message. Then I looked up at Estelle when she walked into the room. "Um, there isn't any way a normal can find out the location of this town, is there?"

"Theoretically, yes, but the town is protected against normals stumbling across it," she said. "Why?"

I showed her the message. "Is there another town called Ivory Beach in the area which isn't magical?"

"Not that I'm aware of." Her brow wrinkled. "I'll ask my mum."

Weird. Off the top of my head, the only way I could think of for a normal to find their way here was if someone else from the magical world told them. I'd been careful not to let anything slip about the town's location, and Laney would definitely have pressed the issue if I'd said anything that hinted at the magical world's existence. Weird.

I put my phone away and returned to the textbook. "Anyway, I've been looking at spells which can be used against vampires, but I don't think magical shields will cut it. What about fire spells?"

"They require really good aim," she said. "Otherwise, they'll damage your surroundings."

"Meaning I'm not to practise in the library."

"Actually, it's fine as long as we stay here in the classroom," she said. "Regular fire can't spread through the library, but this area is set up as a designated practise room, so pretty much anything goes."

"And water?" I asked. "I know they can't cross running water…"

"You can't conjure up a source of water that big with a wand," she said. "You can move an existing source, but that's a tricky spell to master. I can teach you, though, if you like."

"Move an existing source?" I said. "Like when the Grim Reaper walks through the ocean without his feet touching the water?"

"Sort of." She waved her wand and conjured up a glass of water. "Like this."

She waved her wand in a complex twisting motion. The water in the glass moved in swirling patterns, in time with her wand movements. Then she gave a flicking motion and the water leapt up into the air and flew back into the glass without so much as a splash.

"That's pretty cool," I said. "Water's safer than fire. Maybe not much for the books, though."

"Give it a go," she said. "I'll show you again, then you can try."

I watched her wand movements carefully as she demonstrated again, then drew my own wand and copied. The water shifted a little but didn't move like it had when she'd used the spell.

"I guess I need a steadier hand." I gave another twisting wave of my wand, and the water moved a little. "How would I move a larger body of water?"

"With practise," she said. "You could do the same with

biblio-witch magic, but you need to be very good at visualising where you want the water to move."

"Otherwise, I'd end up getting drenched," I said. "Yeah, I figured. I'll stick with this, for now."

I practised some more, while Estelle watched and offered encouragement and suggestions. Halfway through our lesson, Aunt Adelaide called her out to help her find a book, so I continued to practise alone. Despite my best efforts, I couldn't get the water to shift more than an inch. I'd envisioned moving a river around to block a vampire from coming after me, but at this rate, I wouldn't be able to shift so much as a puddle.

I gave my wand an impatient flick. The water shifted to the right and the glass toppled over, spilling its contents all over the desk. *Guess I walked into that one.*

Estelle wasn't back yet, so I picked up the basic magical defence textbook and skimmed through in search of fire spells. The spells for conjuring and banishing fire looked pretty straightforward. The room was already warded, Estelle had said, so I practised the movement for both spells before picking up my wand. *Here goes nothing.*

Wand in hand, I cast the spell. At once, fire flared to life in mid-air, a swath of flames swirling before my eyes. I waved my wand, and the fire moved, while I marvelled at how the flames didn't touch the wooden stick at all. That was magical fire for you.

I twisted my wand in the banishing movement and the flames vanished. Just as I was congratulating myself for a job well done, a shrill alarm sounded, followed by the sound of beating wings.

"Fire!" bellowed Sylvester.

I pushed the door open to address the owl. "There isn't a—"

A sudden deluge of water poured from the ceiling, drenching me in an instant. Since when did the library have a sprinkler system?

I waved my wand in an attempt to turn it off, only for it to fly out of my slippery hand and clatter to the floor.

"FIRE!" yelled the owl.

"There's no fire!" I crouched down to pick up my wand, soaking my knees in the process. Out in the library, the shelves had moved into defensive positions, conjuring up umbrellas to deflect the water from the sprinklers. My coat was drenched, as was my wand. "I put it out as soon as I conjured it."

"The library's magic doesn't know that, you ignorant toadstool," said Sylvester.

"If that's the case, then it didn't react until I'd already put out the fire," I pointed out. "That's a bit late for a defensive spell, isn't it?"

"What are you doing?" Cass walked over to us, her hair dripping wet and her cloak dragging on the soggy carpet. "Don't tell me you were the one who set off the sprinklers."

"I didn't even know we had a sprinkler system," I protested.

"You need a safety setting on your wand like they give to five-year-olds," said Cass. "Why would you start a fire in a library? I thought you had more sense."

"I was learning how to use fire against vampires," I explained.

"Well, try practising outside," she said.

Aunt Candace stormed downstairs. "What is going on?

Who just upended a load of water all over my manuscript? Whoever it is, they're going to pay for it."

Oh, boy.

———

I sat on the sofa in the living room, nursing a mug of hot chocolate. "It was Sylvester, I'm sure of it."

"I believe you," said Estelle. "Cass, though…"

I sipped my hot chocolate. "I'm more worried Aunt Candace will put me on the list of people to kill off in her next book, to be honest."

"True," she said, "but she's killed all of us off at least once. I think my mum holds the record. I remember Aunt Candace had her poisoned in one of her mysteries because she accidentally went over the top with a cleaning spell and wiped one of her notepads clean."

I snorted. "Bet she loved that."

"Let's just say the two of them had fallings-out every other day when Cass and I were kids," she said. "Trust me, this is the most functional our relationship has ever been."

"Hmm." I dug in my pocket when my phone buzzed with a message from Laney. *"You there?"*

Resigned, I typed out a reply. *"Are you sure you found the right Ivory Beach? How?"*

"Google."

Huh? No magical communities showed up in regular search engines. The magical world had their own online network, but since the library scrambled my internet connection at the best of times, I'd never learned much about it. I *did* know that you couldn't just look up the location on a regular GPS.

"Ok. I'll have to ask my aunts if you can come."

Translation: *please don't just show up.* Not that I didn't want to see her, but even if she did make it past the barriers which made the town unseen to most non-magical people, this was a dangerous time for someone like her to show up in town. No way would I let Laney set foot near the library with a potential killer on the loose.

"I can't wait to see the library!"

I looked up at Estelle. "Did you have the chance to ask your mum how Laney might have found out about Ivory Beach?"

"No, but here she is." Estelle turned to the door.

Aunt Adelaide walked into the room. "Someone say my name?"

"Is the water gone?" I asked. "Sorry about that. I didn't know—"

"Think nothing of it," said Aunt Adelaide. "It's far from the only flood we've had here in the library. At least this one didn't come accompanied with a storm like one of Candace's weather spells."

"True," I said. "Aunt Adelaide, is it possible for someone in the normal world to find out our town exists? Laney says she found us.'

"Did you tell her where it was?" asked Aunt Adelaide.

"I assumed there weren't any normal towns in the area with the same name," I said. "Not with a giant library, either. She said *Google* gave her the answer."

"Well, that can't be right," said Aunt Adelaide. "Are you sure your friend is being truthful?"

"She'd have no reason to lie to me."

When we'd last seen one another, she'd seemed the same person she'd been before I'd left her behind. No hints of anything magical. No more than me, anyway, and I had an awful lot more secrets to hide than she did.

"And she hasn't gone on the magical web?" asked Estelle.

"Of course not," I said. "I wouldn't have been able to show her even if I'd wanted to. Does the magical internet ever glitch and randomly become available to outsiders?"

"No," said Aunt Adelaide. "Are you quite certain your friend has no other contacts in the magical world?"

"Not that I'm aware of."

A chill raced through my blood. Either she was lying and had found out another way, or... or someone else from this world had told my best friend where Ivory Beach was. Unless I'd let the location slip, that is, but I doubted I had. I'd been careful.

Aunt Adelaide shot me a concerned look. "Are you seeing her again?"

"She wants to come here," I said. "Still sorting that one out, but I can invite myself to see her again and see if I can do some careful questioning. I just don't want to have to use magic on her or anything."

I wasn't doing myself any favours by poking around in the Vampire Section of the library, either, but if the Founders came here, I needed to be able to protect myself against them. The memory of seeing that vampire on the bridge sent a shiver down my spine that even the warmth of my hot chocolate couldn't dispel. What if I hadn't imagined it? Laney still lived near the site of the vampires' first attack, and if they'd ever been back there, they might well have seen the two of us together. Even keeping my distance might not ensure her safety.

Aunt Adelaide nodded. "I understand, Rory. It's your

choice. As for your magical defence lesson earlier..."

I hung my head. "I'll practise outside next time."

"There's no need." She held out a small pouch. "This might serve you better in a pinch."

I peered into the pouch and nearly dropped it. "Firedust?"

"It's more effective than magic," she said. "No doubt that's why the vampires themselves used it against you. If you find yourself in a situation where you can't access your wand or biblio-witch magic..."

I swallowed down my apprehension. Okay, the vampires had used the firedust to threaten me before, but what better way to face my fear than to use their own weapon against them? "I hope I don't end up in that situation, then. I've already struck 'moving large bodies of water' off the list."

"You'll get better with practise," said Estelle.

"It'd be a lot easier if they couldn't read my thoughts," I said. "Actually, wasn't there a potion which can block mind-reading? That kid used it... Cameron."

A vampire had told him about it, in fact. It had been my first hint that the vampires were recruiting from outside of their immediate circle.

Over my dead body would I let my best friend be one of them.

"We've never seen that potion since then," Estelle said. "Better to stick with the firedust."

Aunt Candace sailed into the room. "If you're looking for an opportunity to test out your skills, Rory, I have just the thing. I've secured us all invitations to a party held at the vampires' church tomorrow, hosted by none other than Evangeline herself."

7

"We're not going," Aunt Adelaide said flatly. "Even if none of these vampires are involved in illicit activity, why would Evangeline invite *us* to a party, anyway?"

They'd been having the same argument for the last day, which always ended on the same note. While Aunt Adelaide refused point-blank to let her sister go alone, the rest of us had considerable reservations about setting foot in the creepy church in which the local vampires made their home.

"Because I explained that I required the advice of a vampire in my research," said Aunt Candace. "I'm writing a historical novel next, and what better way to learn about the 19th century than from someone who lived in it?"

"Why not just ask one of them to come to the library?" I asked. "Seems more logical than wandering onto their territory, where we're totally out of our element."

Literally. Our biblio-witch magic weakened the further we went from the library. And besides, Aunt

Candace never failed to remind us of how much she disliked social events.

"It's open to the public, silly," she said. "We won't be the only witches present."

"We can't all leave the library at the same time," said Aunt Adelaide. "I won't allow it."

"You don't have to come," she said. "By all means, stay here and guard the library yourself, and I'll go on my own. And with Rory, if she wants to speak to the bloodsuckers as well."

"Aunt Candace," I said, "you hate parties. Why did you decide now was a good time to make an exception? I think the vampires will notice if you have your notebook hovering around, besides."

"It's not a party, it's a sophisticated high-society gathering," she said. "Besides, we must make sacrifices for our art."

I rolled my eyes. "I bet Cass won't come either. That leaves Estelle and me."

Estelle, who'd mostly sat out of the family arguments on the subject, chewed on her lower lip. "Aunt Candace, you're not going alone. A vampire *died* the other day. Research opportunity or not, what if the killer *was* one of the vampires from Ivory Beach? They'd only have to read our minds to find out we've been watching the situation. Have you even tried learning how to shield your thoughts?"

"I don't need to," she said. "If the vampires don't like what they see in my head, it's their problem, not mine."

Aunt Adelaide released a breath. "I've made all the arguments I'm willing to make, Candace. If you meet an unfortunate end, it's on your own head."

She walked away, leaving Estelle and me alone with Aunt Candace.

"So dramatic," said Aunt Candace. "Anyone would think there was a madman with a chainsaw on the loose."

"They're vampires," I said. "They don't need to carry chainsaws to be a threat. If one of us came with you, you wouldn't do anything stupid like give us the slip, would you?"

"Not at all." She sauntered away. "If you're coming with me, the party begins at six."

Estelle blew out a breath. "I'll still be dealing with the returns by then. I'll try to get away, but I might be a bit late."

I could see where this was going. I'd already texted Xavier telling him we might have to postpone our date for another night. Given the Grim Reaper's enmity with the vampires, he'd never let his apprentice attend Evangeline's party, so if I went, I'd be stuck with Aunt Candace on my own until Estelle was able to join me.

"I can go with her, but if this goes wrong, I'm not sure the two of us could fend off a whole church full of angry vampires."

"That shouldn't happen," said Estelle. "She'd have to do something *really* bad to anger everyone at the gathering at the same time."

"Like say something questionable to Evangeline?" I queried. "Not sure I can stop her if she's on a roll."

"She claims she just wants to talk to this one guy about 19th century England," said Estelle. "If you go with her, I'll be able to join you within half an hour. If not, then I don't blame you in the slightest."

"Well, I did want to find out if any of the vampires

knew the man who died," I allowed. "I guess I'll also have to occupy Aunt Candace's attention for long enough to stop her from making enemies out of a bunch of blood-sucking immortals."

"If you're certain," she said. "And you have something to wear."

"Ah." What was I even supposed to wear to an event like that? "Pretty sure I don't have anything fancy enough for a vampire party."

"You can borrow one of Cass's dresses," said Estelle. "I think you two are the same size."

I arched a brow. "And she wouldn't mind?"

"She never wears them anyway." She put on a thoughtful expression. "She'll call us idiots for going to this event, but it's worth a shot."

"You've got that right." Cass sauntered into view, wand in hand. "Try this one."

Before I had the chance to object, she gave her wand a flick, and a dress materialised in place of my cloak. I staggered in surprise, disarmed to suddenly find myself wearing a big puffy-sleeved number with lace trimmings. When she conjured up a mirror, I shook my head at my reflection.

"I can't wear this, Cass. I don't think these sleeves will even fit through the doorway."

"All right." Another flick, and I wore a slinky number which exposed enough skin that the vampires would have absolutely no trouble finding somewhere to bite me.

Estelle studied me. "That looks good on you, actually."

"I like it, but I'll be in a freezing church which probably has no heating," I said. "Also, I'd rather my neck was covered. Just, you know, to avoid tempting fate."

"So pedantic." Another flick of Cass's wand conjured a sweeping blue dress with a matching jacket.

"Thank you," I said, surprised to find I liked the look of its shimmering silver-blue colour.

"Try not to spill anything on it," Cass answered. "Like wine. Or blood."

"I'll try not to." My heart squeezed with a spasm of fear, and I gave myself a mental shake. *Relax. It's illegal for any of the vampires to do you harm.* "I wouldn't count on them having beverages on offer which are suitable for humans. We won't be the only humans there, right, Aunt Candace?"

I'd spotted her curly red hair behind a bookshelf, and sure enough, she poked her head out. "Don't be silly. There'll be plenty of other victims. I mean, humans."

"Ha ha."

Really, the biggest risk was that Aunt Candace would go careening back into her vampire phase and end up causing a scene. But I'd be a fool to turn down an opportunity to rub shoulders with the vampires in a safe environment. Safer than usual, anyway.

———

When it came to the moment to leave, I sought out Aunt Adelaide, who sat doing paperwork in the living room.

"Hey." I dug my hand in my bag. "Is it okay if I leave my dad's journal with you? I don't feel comfortable leaving it unattended, but I'm not taking it with me, either."

"Of course." She held out a hand for it. "Rory, are you certain about this?"

Nope. "Estelle will join me after half an hour. I'm taking Jet with me, too."

"If you're sure." She tucked the journal into her pocket. "You do have everything ready, don't you?"

Meaning the firedust. And my wand and Biblio-Witch Inventory. "Of course."

Aunt Candace skipped into the room, wearing a black dress which wouldn't have looked out of place at a funeral. Unlike me, though, she seemed to have no problem whatsoever with leaving her neck bare. "Thought I'd fit with the theme."

"I can tell," said Aunt Adelaide. "What's with the bag?"

Aunt Candace produced a large shoulder bag. "It's for snacks. I get hungry, and I bet the vamps don't have a good selection of snacks on offer for their human guests."

"Or stakes?" I gave her a wary look. "If you're carrying anything which is going to get us both elevated to the top of Evangeline's hit list, I'd leave it behind."

"No stakes." She smiled. "I'm on my best behaviour. Shall we be off?"

Estelle waved goodbye as we walked through the lobby, while Jet swooped down to land on my shoulder before we reached the door.

"Jet, can you do me a favour?" I asked him. "When we get to the vampires' house, I want you to listen out for any mention of the Founders, particularly in relation to my dad's journal. Also, if any of them mention the murder of Rudolph Mint, I need you to tell me, but be careful not to let anyone see or hear you."

I had one advantage: vampires could only read human minds, not animals. Jet would be safe from them suspecting he was spying on them as long as he kept his distance and didn't draw attention.

As for me, I had a task and a half ahead of me if I wanted to keep Aunt Candace from causing trouble. I followed her through the middle of town, shivering in the chill night air as we made our way towards the old church which formed the main headquarters for the town's vampires. Its dark spires pierced the night sky, while the number of smartly dressed figures drifting around the grounds made the place look even more like we'd stepped into a Victorian Gothic novel than it usually did.

Outside the heavy oak doors, Evangeline greeted everyone who entered, wearing a stunning black dress and vibrant blood-red lipstick. Her hair ran in curls like a waterfall, her skin was as pale as porcelain, and she looked every inch the vampire queen she was.

Evangeline smiled at me. "It's a pleasure to see you, Aurora."

"You too," I lied. Jet shivered on my shoulder, hiding himself in my hair until I got close enough to the doors for him to flit inside.

Aunt Candace grinned at the vampires' leader. "Why, hello, Evangeline."

Evangeline's expression turned frosty. "Candace Hawthorn. I'm afraid I'm going to have to ask if I can search your bag."

Aunt Candace opened her bag to show the leading vampire. "See? It's just snacks. I had a feeling this event wouldn't provide for its human guests."

"I see." Her sharp gaze raked over the contents of the bag. "You were correct. See to it that you don't make a mess."

She stepped aside, and we walked through the towering oak doors into the church. It looked just as impressive on the inside as it did on the outside, with wide stone floors, stained-glass windows, and pillars supporting the high, arched ceilings. As I'd suspected, the church had little in the way of central heating for its human guests, and my breath fogged the air in front of me.

I spotted Jet flying around listening out for gossip, but I felt oddly exposed without him. It didn't help that I didn't know anyone here. While Aunt Candace and I weren't the only humans present, I was conscious of the eerily beautiful people forming the vast majority of the crowd. I did my best to make myself as small and incon-spicuous as possible, but with Aunt Candace at my side, that was a tall order.

"Lord Vogel!" she said loudly, her voice echoing. Everyone in the vicinity turned our way as she walked over to a tall, pale vampire wearing a fitted suit. "Good to see you."

"Ah, Candace," he said. "I'm glad you could make it."

"Oh, I wouldn't miss the chance to talk to someone who lived through the Victorian era," she said. "Can you regale me with some tales of your fascinating life?"

The vampire launched into a long anecdote which went way over my head, with Aunt Candace listened intently. Shivering with cold, I stepped back and startled when Jet landed on my shoulder.

"That man over there mentioned the murder of Rudolph Mint!" he squeaked in my ear. "He said he thinks a non-vampire did it."

I squinted into the darkness to find the person he'd

pointed out and frowned in confusion when it became apparent that the man in question was human. Not a vampire. Perhaps a wizard, though he wore the same smart attire as the rest of the crowd.

I drew in a deep breath and walked in his direction, sticking to the shadows. He was talking to a woman of around my age—also human. With a flick of my wand, I cast a camouflage spell to make myself unseen. While any vampire might still pick up on my presence, a human who wasn't paying attention wouldn't notice me.

"I can't believe she's holding a party at a time like this," the man was saying to his companion. "A vamp dies by stake—minutes from here—and she acts as though it doesn't matter."

"It doesn't," the woman replied. "Not to her. She's secure in her wealth and power."

"So was Rudolph Mint and it didn't make a difference to him," said the man. "She must know there's a high risk."

"Relax. If we stay on her good side, we'll have her protection."

Confusion flared in the back of my mind. Why in the world would two humans expect to have Evangeline's protection? Like all vampires, she wasn't concerned with anyone outside of her own immediate circle, let alone anyone who had a pulse.

It didn't sound like the two humans thought Evangeline was responsible for the murder, either, come to that. I inched closer, hoping to hear more, but an exclamation from behind me made me spin around on the spot. I expected to see Aunt Candace at the centre, but instead, three vampires surrounded another, shorter figure, who cowered away from them.

"He said I could bite him!" the vampire said indignantly, reaching for the cowering human.

"Seward, let him go," said Evangeline. "No biting the guests."

Good to know there were house rules. Just when I was debating leaving Aunt Candace to her questioning and taking off alone, I spotted Estelle hovering near the entrance. Relieved to see a friendly face, I pulled out my wand and undid the camouflage spell before approaching Estelle. "Hey."

"How's it going?" she asked.

"Surprisingly, not too bad," I said. "Aunt Candace is talking that vampire's ear off. Someone just tried to bite a human, if you saw, but they're supposed to be on their best behaviour."

"I should hope so," said Estelle. "You got in with no trouble?"

"Aside from Evangeline getting suspicious about all the snacks Aunt Candace brought and insisting on searching her bag?"

"Are you sure that's why she did it?" she asked. "Might she have been looking for... you know."

Good point. Had she been looking for the journal? Maybe she'd assumed I'd given it to Aunt Candace for safekeeping and hadn't left it behind. She knew I didn't trust her, after all. But then, why would she think I'd brought it at all? Unless she assumed that I didn't go anywhere without it, but that was just guesswork.

"Anyway, there's something I wanted to ask about..." I dropped my voice as two vampires walked past. "There are humans over there, and it sounds like they're close friends with the vampires." I explained what I'd heard. "Why would humans want Evangeline's protection?"

"Her protection?" she echoed. "Maybe they want to be turned into vampires. New vamps are closely monitored, but it's not unheard of them to recruit humans as subjugates by luring them in with the promise of becoming one of them."

I'd got that impression from the book I'd read, too. Perhaps they belonged to an adult version of the Aspiring Vampires Society which had once been all the rage at the local academy before we'd banned their group from meeting in the library.

"Why would witches and wizards want to become vampires?"

"For any reason," she said. "It can happen, you know. People romanticise vampires."

"I gathered." I shivered. "I'm also regretting not wearing my cloak. I should have figured they wouldn't have this place set up for our comfort."

"You aren't wrong," she said. "I'll ask Aunt Candace if she'll be done soon."

I made to follow her, but Evangeline barred my path, her tall figure towering over me. "I heard you spoke to Mr Vale."

I tensed. "From whom?"

Ignoring my question, she said, "Why, pray tell, would you willingly meet with someone who threatened your life?"

"I wanted to ask him something," I said, careful to keep my thoughts blank. "About the Founders. Since the murder victim was part of their group, I wondered if others might be in the area."

Her mouth pulled with distaste. "Mortimer Vale has not set foot outside the jail since his imprisonment began. Why would you believe he'd know anything about the Founders' movements?"

"He pays attention," I said. "He confirmed he and Rudolph Mint were acquainted."

Interest stirred in her expression. "So he did agree to speak to you. It seems I underestimated you, Aurora."

I remained silent for a moment. Mortimer Vale and I were as far from friends as it was possible to be, but I hadn't the faintest idea where she stood on the matter of our acquaintance. It depended whether she was part of the Founders herself or not.

"Did you ever meet before he came to town?" I asked. "I know you've both lived a long time... like a lot of the guests here."

"Oh, yes, it's a hazard of being one of us." She smiled. "Grudges can last centuries. One of the few downsides to immortality."

"Do you think that might be why Rudolph Mint died? A grudge?"

"I doubt it," she said. "He died by staking—imperfectly, at that. Not a method used by my kind against one another."

So she believed the same as those two humans did... that the killer hadn't been a vampire at all. From her tone, I assumed Evangeline didn't know or like the victim, but those two humans had a point. It seemed in poor taste to throw a party with a potential vampire killer on the loose in town.

"Do you think..." I hesitated. "I mean, do you think a vampire hunter might be in town?"

"If there was, I'd know." She gave me a piercing look. "Why, you don't suspect anyone, do you? Did Vale tell you anything?"

"Not that I could make much sense out of," I said. "He was more interested in getting under my skin."

"I suppose he would have been," she said. "A vampire hunter wouldn't have missed the heart."

"Missed?" I echoed.

Wait a moment. When a vampire was staked through the heart, they turned to dust. For Rudolph Mint's body to have shown up in one piece meant the killer hadn't hit his heart. That made it even less likely to have been a vampire. Or a vampire hunter. Staking a vampire and leaving their body intact meant leaving evidence behind, whereas if the dead vampire had turned to dust, nobody would have known he was dead.

Behind Evangeline, I spotted Estelle beckoning frantically to me from beside Aunt Candace. I took a step towards her. Then, a sudden burst of screaming drifted in from a gap in the oak doors. It echoed off the high ceilings, causing all heads to turn towards the entrance.

"Someone's dead!" shouted a voice.

Everyone ran to the doors in a tide of trampling feet. Estelle and I were pushed to the back, and it was several seconds before we saw the woman in a red dress standing beside the bushes outside the front door, jabbing a finger at the shadows beneath the window.

"He's dead," the woman said. "Look…"

Evangeline glided through the crowd, which parted like water. She lifted the limp body out of the bush, exposing the stake thrust through the man's ribcage.

8

For a moment, everyone was silent. The vampire's body hung limp in Evangeline's hands, unmistakably dead.

"The stake missed his heart." Evangeline placed his body back on the ground.

Missed his heart? Like the first victim? Murmurs broke out among the crowd as the same conclusion occurred to them, too. Then, everyone froze as the leader of the vampires exposed her fangs, casting a furious glare around the gathering guests.

"There will be blood for this," she said. "I will not allow anyone to leave until I find who committed this crime on my property."

"What?" said one of the other vampires. "That's hardly fair. The killer might have come in from outside."

"Did I give you permission to speak?" Evangeline enquired. "I don't think so. Everyone, go back into the church. *Now.*"

We found ourselves unceremoniously herded back

into the church. I ended up backed into a corner while Evangeline swooped around, ordering each person to come forward one at a time so she could read their thoughts. Most vampires could read other vamps' minds, in theory, but they were also well-practised in locking their thoughts against their fellow vampires. Then again, Evangeline had more skill than most. Even if she deemed someone innocent, she still refused to let them leave, with the result that the walls echoed with the complaints of disgruntled vampires and non-vampires alike.

Estelle caught my arm and whispered in my ear, "Some people are sneaking out the back way. If we don't get out soon, we'll be in here all night."

I knew that, but someone was dead—which meant the Reaper wouldn't be far behind. On the other hand, Evangeline seemed no closer to finding the culprit, and I was inclined to agree with the vampire who'd suggested the killer had come in from outside and was long gone by now.

"All right," I whispered. "Jet's in here. I hope he knows we're sneaking out."

We wove our way through the church to a door at the back, where a steady line of guests made a stealthy exit. I glanced up as a small shape flitted overhead. "It's Jet. I'll be right behind you."

Estelle hauled Aunt Candace after her out of the church while I waited for the crow to land on my shoulder.

"It's them!" he squeaked. "They're coming this way."

I wheeled around on the spot. The two humans from earlier were on their way to the exit, too. Checking to make sure Estelle had Aunt Candace under her watch, I stepped out of line to whisper, "Jet, did you hear or see anything that would suggest anyone here at the party killed that guy?"

"No, partner. I was listening for any mention of the Founders, but I heard nothing about this grievous killing."

"Okay," I whispered. "I'm going to follow them. Can you keep quiet and watch out for trouble?"

"Yes, partner!"

I waved my wand and cast the camouflage spell again, then followed the two humans out of the exit. Jet flew silently behind, while I slowed my pace as I drew closer to the strangers.

"This was unfortunate," muttered the man.

"What did she expect?" the woman hissed back. "She opened the event to the public with a killer on the loose."

"If not for the event being open to the public, *we* wouldn't have got in," he responded. "They barely let vampires from outside their territory in. Let alone… what did they call us? Normals."

My spine stiffened. The two strangers were *normals?* Why would Evangeline have ordinary, non-magical normals at her party? How had they known Ivory Beach existed at all?

"Did you call the taxi, at least?" the woman asked. "I'm not leaving until I'm sure we won't run into trouble on the way back."

"Relax, Jean," said the man. "They're looking for vampires, not people like us. The taxi will drop us off at the bridge, near Cobb Street…"

Ice slid down my spine. Cobb Street was near where I used to work. They were from the same area as Laney. A normal town, with zero magical connections.

They'd come here to Ivory Beach just for the party. Why would they take that risk? Who'd promised them they'd be safe? And who, exactly, had told them about the magical world to begin with?

"Good, because I'm not walking alone at night," said the woman. "Even with the protective charm, there's something not right about these deaths. They said we'd be safe…"

Protective charm? Who'd given the normals something to keep themselves safe? Who'd *want* them around the vampires? Even when they were on their best behaviour, vampires were volatile and dangerous, and all humans were out of their depth. Magical or otherwise.

Someone in the area was sharing information about the magical world with normals. People like Laney. She wasn't at the party—thank god—but that didn't mean she was safe. After all, we might have been seen together when I'd visited my old neighbourhood, or even before then. Who knew what the unscrupulous vampires might do next?

I made to follow the humans out the gates, but a shadow fell across the path. A long, cold shadow attached to a tall figure clothed in back.

The Grim Reaper was here. I hurried out of sight as he swooped down the path towards the church, my heart thumping in my chest. So he hadn't sent his apprentice. Given how the victim was a vampire, I should have expected him to come in person, but that put an end to any plans I might have of picking up any clues about who'd murdered one of Evangeline's guests. I wouldn't do myself any favours by drawing Evangeline's attention again, so I caught up to Estelle at the back gate. Aunt

Candace walked ahead of us, her notebook and pen hovering at her side.

"There you are," Estelle said. "What kept you?"

"Those two humans." I dropped my voice. "They were *normals,* and not from Ivory Beach at all. They didn't know Evangeline. Someone else invited them here, but I don't know who."

"Normals?" Her eyes rounded. "Are you sure?"

"They didn't see me eavesdropping on them, so they must have been telling the truth," I said. "I'd ask Evangeline, but the Grim Reaper's on his way to pick up the victim's soul and I didn't think he'd appreciate it if I interrupted him."

"He didn't send Xavier?"

"Apparently not," I murmured. "Not only that, the vampire was staked imperfectly. Not through the heart. Because of that, Evangeline doesn't think it was a vampire hunter *or* another vampire who killed Rudolph Mint. I'm assuming her theory hasn't changed for this victim either, given that she seemed to think one of her guests was the culprit when we spoke earlier."

"Oh, is that what you were talking about?" she said. "I'm surprised she talked to you."

"She never passes up an opportunity to needle me," I said. "She seemed surprised that I spoke to Mortimer Vale."

"Of course she heard about that, too," said Estelle. "Be careful, Rory."

"It's not like I broadcasted our meeting to the whole town." I huddled inside my jacket, shivering. "If anything, she was more helpful than he was. He might pretend to be all-knowing, but he hasn't left the jail. He seemed livid over Rudolph Mint's death. Not sure if he knew the latest victim."

"You definitely don't suspect her anymore?" she murmured. "Evangeline?"

"I'm not sure I do." I walked on, catching up to Aunt Candace. "What about the guy you were talking to? Get in any pertinent questions about the murders?"

"I might have got to that part if *someone* hadn't interrupted me." She cast a disgruntled look at Estelle.

"Don't blame me, blame the killer," said Estelle. "You'd better hope the vampires didn't see your notebook and pen."

Jet landed on my shoulder. "Evangeline is angry that half her guests sneaked out through the back door."

"I hope you got a lot of information out of your meeting, Aunt Candace," said Estelle. "Because I doubt we'll get another invitation to a vampire gathering anytime soon."

"Good," I said. "I think we're done risking our necks for a long while."

———

We reached the library without encountering any vampires, thankfully. Aunt Candace opened the door first and disappeared to the living quarters without further ado. Estelle and I followed her and found Aunt Adelaide waiting for us in the living room.

"Quiet night?" I asked Aunt Adelaide.

"Someone tried to get past the library's defences," she said. "They vanished by the time I got downstairs."

"What—someone tried to break in?" My heart lurched. "Did you see them?"

"No, but the doors were locked, so they must have given up," she replied. "Of course, it might have just been someone trying to return a book."

"Really?" said Estelle, in sceptical tones. "Wasn't someone watching the door? Like Sylvester?"

"He took charge of the ground floor," said Aunt Adelaide. "Whoever tried to get in didn't make any sound or cause a disturbance, so it wasn't apparent to any of us until I unlocked the doors ready for your return and saw that someone had tried to force their way past the security spells."

Estelle's brow crinkled. "They didn't use magic?"

"Apparently not," she said. "What happened at the party? I heard a commotion."

"Someone died," said Estelle. "A vampire. Evangeline lost her mind and locked the church doors to question everyone. She'd have kept us in there all night if we hadn't sneaked out the back way."

"You sneaked out?" said Aunt Adelaide.

"It was that or let Aunt Candace ask the wrong questions and get us all arrested." I gave my aunt a pointed look when she exited the kitchen with a mug of hot chocolate. "You still haven't said if you learned anything useful from Lord Vogel. And did you know there were normals at the party?"

"Normals?" she echoed. "No, I didn't. How very foolish of them."

"I followed two of them and listened to their conversation," I added, for Aunt Adelaide's benefit. "They *knew* about our world. They also didn't seem surprised that someone died. It sounded like the vampires gave them some kind of protective charm. Who'd invite normals to a party in a town like this?"

Aunt Adelaide frowned. "I'll look into the matter. Candace, were you on your best behaviour?"

"What kind of question is that?" Aunt Candace tutted. "I got some *astounding* research into secret societies and historical issues from Lord Vogel."

"Was *he* one of the Founders?" I turned on her, a wave of suspicion rising.

"He used to be," she said. "Most of the older vampires were initially part of the Founders. It's a small number compared to the vampires who exist now. He hasn't been involved with their activities in recent years."

"Really, Candace," said Aunt Adelaide. "Did it not occur to you that someone involved with the Founders is murdering people?"

"It's irrelevant." She waved her hand. "Lord Vogel is on his way home now, besides. He was only in town for a short while."

"Unless Evangeline locks everyone in the vampires' church indefinitely until she finds the killer," I added. "I'm starting to think those normals had a point. She didn't pick the best time to hold a party."

Evangeline thought herself invincible... which she almost was. But it was Laney who concerned me. Laney, and those two normals who'd willingly stepped into our world. Or rather, who'd been led here by someone they trusted.

If a vampire had told *her* about the magical world... but surely she would have mentioned it to me if they had. In any case, I had to make sure she was safe, but I couldn't watch her all the time, especially from here.

It seemed my only option was to invite her to the library, while keeping my fingers crossed that the paranormal world's dangers hadn't already reached her.

———

It wasn't until after a near-sleepless night that I remembered that I hadn't asked Aunt Adelaide for my dad's journal back. I'd tossed and turned for hours, pondering how to handle the situation with Laney and ruminating on everything Jet had told me he'd overheard from the guests—which didn't add up to anything concrete about the killer's identity.

After I'd showered and dressed, I went looking for Aunt Adelaide, but she wasn't in the living room. Instead, I found Sylvester perched on top of a cabinet.

"Oh," I said. "Hey. Is Aunt Adelaide around?"

The owl rotated his head to face the wall, in the most passive-aggressive gesture I'd ever seen from a bird in my life.

"Look, you're going to have to forgive me someday," I said.

"Not at all," he replied. "I can hold a grudge for the rest of your life if I feel like it."

"As long as the vampires?" I queried. "Wait, how old are you?"

He'd been around since Grandma had opened the library. Not quite as old as the vampires, but impressive for an owl.

"None of your business, whippersnapper," he said. "As for the vampires, most of their grudges end in bloodshed."

"Like last night," I said. "I suppose you heard about the attempted break-in? Weren't you watching?"

He hooted. "They never got past the doors."

"Sounds like they did a good job of trying to break them down," I commented. "Then again, I'm surprised nobody tried to take refuge here after they escaped the party. Especially the normals."

I'd hoped that might get his attention and cause him to forget his grudge, but he clucked his beak in disapproval. "Foolish normals have always been enticed by the vampires' world. It never ends well for them."

"Aren't you a bit concerned about them drawing attention to the magical world?" I asked. "And getting us all into trouble?"

"Are you volunteering to deal with them yourself?" he enquired. "If I was concerned about normals causing trouble, then I'd have chased you out on the first day you arrived here. Perhaps I should have done exactly that."

"Thanks," I said. "And I'm not talking about people like me, who have family in the magical world. I'm talking about normals who would willingly accept an invitation to a vampire's party without any concern for their own safety *or* the magical world's secrecy. Have you heard about anything like that?"

"Since I wasn't invited, I wouldn't know."

"Sylvester, you were nowhere to be seen yesterday," I said. "Did you really want to come to a vampire party, anyway?"

I knew what his issue was this time. He always got annoyed whenever I reminded him that his knowledge, however vast, was limited to the inside of the library itself and not anything that happened outside it.

"I was engaged in important work within the library," he said. "Which the rest of you seem to have forgotten about."

"We were trying to protect the library," I pointed out. "From a killer. Do you think it was anyone from town?"

"I wasn't there, and besides, I'm not talking to you."

"They might come here next," I added. "How would you feel if my body showed up drained of blood, and you had to live with the knowledge that you never forgave me while I was still alive?"

"I don't respond to emotional manipulation," said the owl.

Worth a shot. I did have some theories about the killer, but nothing concrete enough to pin on anyone in particular, let alone from within the town itself. I was fairly certain it wasn't Evangeline by now, but I doubted she'd be thrilled if I turned up to ask her how last night's questioning had ended.

Aunt Adelaide entered the living room and held out my dad's journal. "Here, Rory. I gave it another go with the translator spell last night, just in case."

I took the journal gratefully and put it back into my shoulder bag. "Any luck?"

"No, but I did find some interesting research on the Founders," she said. "It seems they don't see normals the way the rest of magical society does. They believe normals and magical folk should be free to intermingle as they please."

"That's because they think of all of us as a food source." Aunt Candace poked her head into the room, her hair uncombed and a frilly, flowery dressing gown swirling around her ankles. "Why bother being picky?"

"She isn't wrong," Aunt Adelaide said as her sister withdrew her head and ambled into the kitchen. "Witches and wizards are less inclined to submit to being used as a feeding source for a vampire than regular humans are. Also, vampires are more able to adapt to living in human towns and cities than the rest of us."

I suppressed a shiver. To vampires, human blood and witch blood tasted the same, and we were equally vulnerable. No wonder some of them didn't see any difference between us.

"Doesn't mean they're allowed to break the paranormal laws and invite normals to their parties," I said. "Is it likely that the magical authorities will find out?"

"No." Her lips pursed. "I doubt any of the normals are responsible for the two deaths. They wouldn't have the ability to overcome a vampire."

"Except the person who did it missed the heart," I added. "Which suggests it wasn't a vampire, either."

"Unless they wanted to leave a message behind," said Aunt Adelaide. "If staked in the heart, a vampire turns to dust. There'd be no traces remaining. If the killer wanted the bodies to be found…"

"Then they wanted to ensure the local vamps found them?" I frowned. "But—which vampire? Someone who doesn't like Evangeline, evidently, but that would cover a lot of people. Especially after last night. I guess going back to talk to her again is out of the question until she calms down."

The town as a whole might end up in a lot of trouble if the magical authorities got wind of normals being invited to a vampires' gathering, and I couldn't help wondering how they'd received the invitation to begin with. Perhaps

I should talk to the two humans, but I didn't know whereabouts they lived, only that it was close to Laney's home and my former neighbourhood.

"I would advise you to avoid Evangeline for the foreseeable future," Aunt Adelaide said. "I believe she sent out the invitations to every vampire in her circle and others outside of it, so I suppose some of them must have taken that as an invitation to bring their human companions along."

"And given them protective charms," I added. "They're recruiting from among normals, but it didn't sound like those two knew who the killer was. Not sure if they've ever met Mortimer Vale either."

"The Founders' group hasn't always had the same members, and many of them have left in the last few decades," said Aunt Adelaide. "Like that gentleman Candace interviewed."

"That's why I wondered if Evangeline might be involved with them," I said. "She's interested in the journal, but it might not mean she's buddies with Mortimer Vale."

Dominic had left me a note warning me not to show her the journal, but that might be due to her intentions to possess the journal for herself rather than implicating her in a crime. She might be unscrupulous, but I doubted she'd murdered someone at her own party.

"Whatever the journal's contents, your father all but vampire-proofed them," she said.

"And human-proofed them, too," I said. "I wonder... was it one of the normals who tried to break into the library? A vampire wouldn't have given up so easily."

"Perhaps," she said. "It's unpleasant, Rory, but humans

who end up involved in vampire society are often manip-ulated into taking risks and doing things the vampires wouldn't want to dirty their hands with. Normals have even fewer natural defences than we do. As it says in that *Vampire Defence* book..."

I shuddered. "When I got that book out, I was under the impression it was supposed to teach me how to defend myself against vampires, not the other way around. Though maybe I should have stuck with that one over summoning fire in the library."

"You had the right idea," she said. "You can infer more than you might expect about vampires from studying their own texts."

"A vampire wrote the book." I should have guessed that from the first chapter. "I didn't read all of it."

"The book details how humans can be turned into subjugates via a vampire's bite without becoming a vampire themselves," she said. "The various ways vampires can make a human dependent on them are... extensive. Did the two you saw at the party seem fatigued, dazed, and unnaturally devoted to the vampires around them?"

"Honestly, no," I said. "That means they weren't bitten, right? They mentioned someone giving them a protective charm."

"Yes, I looked those up," she said. "I believe they might have been carrying a charm which can make a human immune to a vampire's bite, but such charms don't quell the side effects of drinking a vampire's blood."

"Drinking their blood is required for them to turn into a vampire, right?" I said. "They have to be bitten and *then* drink their blood, or else they won't turn."

"Or the other way around," she said. "Drinking the blood of a vampire creates a bond between the two which is all but involuntary on the human's part. It also bestows some vampire-like powers on the human, including enhanced senses and minor boosts to their speed and strength. But the effects fade quickly unless they keep drinking. It's also highly addictive if it's drank frequently enough. Like caffeine or alcohol."

I grimaced. "Yeah, no thanks. So some vampires purposefully give their own blood to humans to make them dependent on them?"

"Unfortunately," she said. "It's difficult to detect, and since most vampires have a superior position among other paranormals, it usually falls to them to track down their own transgressors. That means the crime goes largely unnoticed."

Those two humans had seemed fine, but it bothered me that nobody had questioned them being there. Including Evangeline, unless she simply didn't care if any of her guests were in a vampire's thrall.

In the end, I hadn't needed to use my anti-vampire defence training at all… but that didn't mean I wouldn't in future. If, say, I wanted to protect my best friend from becoming their next victim.

I'd take no chances next time. It was time to Laney-proof the library.

9

I began with an assessment of the library from the ground floor. If all the doors to the troublemaking books were locked and anything out of place was stacked away, all I had to do was stop Laney from wandering out of my sight and I just might be able to keep her from getting into trouble.

That is, if I could get the library to cooperate with me… and persuade my family not to use any magic in front of Laney.

"It'll have to be on a weekend," I said to Estelle. "Next weekend, maybe."

"Works for me," said Estelle. "I can hold off on using magic for a day or two. Aunt Candace probably won't leave her room, and as long as Cass's animals are on their best behaviour, we'll be in the clear."

"Just as long as I get her into the library without running into anyone outside."

There was just one slight issue: if Laney was already

on the vampires' radar, then waiting until the following weekend to invite her to visit might be leaving it too late. It didn't help that my phone signal had disappeared again, leaving our communication lines cut off.

"If it's a Sunday morning, nobody will be around anyway." Estelle faced the shelves and made a sweeping gesture, and they moved to the side. "There, try that."

I faced the bookshelves and held up my Biblio-Witch Inventory, pressing my fingertip to the word *move.*

The shelves stubbornly refused to budge. I hung my head. "I guess the library thinks you're more senior than I am."

Estelle pursed her lips. "I still think you should take Laney somewhere other than the library. Or Ivory Beach as a whole."

"I think I was doomed from the instant I mentioned there was a library at all," I admitted. "I mean, if our positions were reversed, I'd be mildly annoyed if I found out she'd been hiding a secret library from me, magical or otherwise. Granted, she isn't quite as obsessive over books as I am, but still."

"The important thing is to make sure she's safe, right?" She lowered her wand. "Hey—Xavier's here."

I abandoned the bookshelves and crossed the lobby to greet my boyfriend. He caught me in a hug, and I wrapped my arms around him. "Hey."

"I was worried about you." He released me. "My boss didn't tell me about the vampire's death until he got back at dawn."

"He just walked out without telling you where he was going?" I asked.

"He does that a lot," he commented. "It's usually work-related, but I should have guessed something would go wrong at the party. Gathering a large number of vampires in one place when someone was already killed in the region struck me as a risky move."

"Not just vampires," I said. "Humans, too. Including normals."

His brows shot up, and he listened with concern as I told him everything from my conversation with Evangeline to what I'd learned from eavesdropping on those humans.

Xavier was quiet for a moment after I'd finished. "So you don't think Evangeline was responsible for the murder."

"She was furious," I said. "Also, I don't see her murdering someone at her own party."

"How do you know for certain?" he said. "She might well have held the event to draw her targets to town, if there were that many non-locals present."

"Since when were you Team Evangeline Is Guilty?"

"Since my boss started badmouthing her all the time," he said. "When he returned last night, he mentioned that she didn't seem grieved by the man's death, more annoyed at her guests for not cooperating with her questioning."

"She locked us in the church and interrogated us," I said. "Anyway, I don't trust her, but from what I overheard from those humans, they think she was foolish to hold the party at all with a killer on the loose in the area."

"The humans might believe she wasn't responsible, but others might disagree," he said. "If they were normals, they don't know our world, and I doubt they know Evangeline, either."

"Neither did I, at first," I said. "I still can't claim to know the intricacies of how the vampires work, but it seems they're more into inviting humans to mingle with them than I realised. Normals or otherwise. I'd have liked to ask Evangeline if she knew there were people from outside the magical world among her guests, but I bet she's still mad at me for sneaking out of the church through the back door."

His brow crinkled. "Yes, I wouldn't visit her for a while. But I do have an alternative."

"What kind of alternative?" I asked. "At the moment, I'm more concerned with keeping my best friend safe from them—which is why I'm trying to get the library to de-magic itself. Needless to say, it's not going well."

Concern flickered across his expression. "You want to bring your best friend here at a time like this?"

"I don't think I have a choice." My hands fisted. "Xavier... she knows where Ivory Beach is. Someone told her. And... and those two normals I saw last night were from the same town I used to live in."

He swore softly under his breath. "You think one of the vampires told her?"

"I hope *not*." Nausea rose in my throat. "Either way, at least if she's here in the library, I can keep an eye on her and maybe ask her to tell me in confidence if a vampire tried to recruit her. If those two humans at the party came from the same area Laney lives in... I can't see it being a coincidence. Nobody magical lives there at all."

But did they target the area because I used to live there?

He cast his gaze around the library. "I understand, Rory, but are you sure inviting her to come to the library is the best plan?"

"No, but it's all I've got," I said. "You still haven't said what your 'alternative' is. To talking to Evangeline, I mean."

"My boss," he said. "He knows more about the vampires than anyone within their ranks."

Huh? "Xavier, your boss hates me."

"He doesn't hate you," he said. "He just treats you with the same indifference as most humans."

I snorted. "Yeah, but I'm a particular annoyance because I keep luring his apprentice away from him. Is this really a good idea? Last time I showed up, he kicked me out."

"This is different," he said. "My boss knows you aren't one of Evangeline's underlings. He won't tell me about the Founders—"

"Then why on earth do you think he'd tell *me?*" I said incredulously. "I'm human. Not a Reaper. Besides, you said he'd never let you reap a vampire's soul."

"Yet," he added. "It's mostly because it's so rare for one to die. But I think it's worth asking him about it."

"Will it bother him that there are normals finding out about this world?" I said. "I wouldn't have thought it would be Reaper business."

After all, the Reapers were a world apart from the rest of us, almost in a literal sense. They operated outside of the usual paranormal laws and had no reason to fear for their freedom if the authorities came snooping. My family, on the other hand, had everything to lose.

"I'll ask him," Xavier said. "If he says no, then you won't have to worry. If yes, then I'll see if he's willing to tell you what he knows about the vampires."

"Thanks," I said. "I appreciate it."

First the vampires and now the Grim Reaper. I was setting records for conquering fears this week. Admittedly, I didn't really expect him to say yes. The Grim Reaper was mildly disdainful towards me at best and showed his disapproval at my dating Xavier at every opportunity.

Xavier left the library, at which point Cass popped up behind the desk.

"You're still bringing your friend to town, even after yesterday?" Cass said. "Don't think I didn't hear all about the murder at Evangeline's get-together."

"I expected you would," I said. "Did you see the break-in last night?"

"I was watching the upper floors," she said. "I didn't hear anything outside."

Meaning, she was with her animals. "Some vampires in the same town I used to live in are recruiting normals. I intend to make sure my best friend doesn't become a target."

"And you think she'd freak out any less over the library than a bunch of sexy vampires?" she said. "Are you taking her to your interview with the Grim Reaper, too?"

"Don't be ridiculous," I said. "He reaped the souls of the two murder victims. He'll know if they had anything to say which might implicate a particular person in their deaths."

She raised a brow. "And you think he'll tell you?"

"First time for everything."

Sylvester swooped down to land on the desk and addressed Cass. "The pixie opened the door on the third floor again."

"I'll sort it," she said. "Bloody pixie."

"Sylvester—" I began, but the owl took off before I could begin to figure out how to finish my sentence.

"Don't you think Sylvester probably opened the door himself?" I said to Cass instead.

She shrugged. "Probably, but I have to humour him. He feels everyone has been ignoring him since the pixie showed up."

"Is that why he's being such a drama queen?" He was still being nice to Cass, but the owl liked her better than the rest of us put together.

My phone buzzed with a message from Xavier: *My boss agreed to speak to you at five this evening.*

My heart gave a nervous flip. Then I hit respond: *OK.*

———

It was time for my interview with the Grim Reaper. Already, the sky had turned inky black, which wasn't unusual for five in the evening at this time of year, but it didn't make me feel any less apprehensive about walking to the local cemetery. Even if the person I was going to see was scarier than anything that might walk out of the graves.

Xavier led the way through the rusty iron gates, which gave an ominous creak as they closed behind me. The chill air penetrated my coat, growing colder the further we walked through the maze of shadowy gravestones lit only by the faint glow of the moon and stars above.

I'd never felt the place fit with Xavier's comparatively sunny personality, and he looked particularly incongruous next to the dark-bricked building located at the back of the cemetery. I'd never been further than the doors before, and a fresh wave of apprehension hit me when we halted at the doorstep.

An old-fashioned door knocker hung in front of us, but Xavier ignored it, instead pushing on the door until it opened.

"Isn't it locked?" I asked.

"Nobody but a Reaper would be able to do that," he told me. "He's waiting inside."

A dark corridor beckoned, and I hesitated on the threshold, willing my racing heart to calm down. Suppressing the instinct to run away, I stepped into the hallway and followed Xavier to a room which contained a long table surrounded by carved wooden chairs which looked more like medieval torture devices than furniture.

The Grim Reaper sat at the end of the table, his dark cloak surrounding his shadowy form and his face masked in shadow. "Aurora Hawthorn."

"Grim Reaper." I swallowed hard, trying to mask my nerves. "You wanted to speak to me?"

"I agreed to this meeting at my apprentice's insistence, despite my reservations," he said. "He seemed convinced you had important information to discuss with me regarding the vampires."

"I do." I took a seat next to Xavier. The wooden chair was as cold and uncomfortable as it looked. "I know you heard about the death at Evangeline's party yesterday because you were called to reap the soul of the person who died. As it's the second death of a vampire in a short space of time, I wondered if... if you'd heard anything from either of the victims which might suggest who was responsible for the crime."

The temperature seemed to drop several degrees,

which was saying a lot, considering the room was already freezing.

"And what, pray tell, suggests that I'm willing to tell you confidential information about the souls I escorted into the afterworld?" he said in a voice like chilled steel.

"Nothing," I croaked. "I mean... I thought you might have information that might prevent there being another victim."

Why had I agreed to this again? Even Xavier sat still beneath his boss's forbidding presence. Perhaps he was having second thoughts, too. But I'd come here for a reason.

"Also," I pressed on, when answers weren't forthcoming. "I thought it might interest you to know that the local vampires are inviting normals to their social events. Some of them are even recruiting people to join their cause from outside the paranormal world."

"What gives you that idea?" he said.

Taking his words as an invitation, I gave him a summary of what I'd overheard between the two humans at the party.

"Those two normals came here with the vampires," I finished. "They came here to Ivory Beach, maybe expecting to be turned into vampires themselves. Considering the Founders have been in the area recently, it's not a stretch to assume they might have been responsible. I don't know if it connects to the two deaths yet, but they still have yet to find the culprit."

"And why should this concern me?" he asked.

"Shouldn't it?" I said. "Doesn't it bother you that the Founders might be recruiting humans and breaking the magical laws? The first victim was on the run from jail when he died."

"That may be, but the vampires have no interest in me, and I have no interest in them," said the Grim Reaper. "If they want to put the secrecy of the magical world at risk, that's their prerogative."

That figured. He and Xavier could disappear any time they wanted to, as he'd already demonstrated to me. Small mercy that *he* wasn't a mind-reader, and therefore couldn't know about our excursion earlier this week.

The Grim Reaper raised his head as a hollow, booming knock echoed from the hallway. What were the odds of another person deciding to meet with the Grim Reaper at the same time as me? I wasn't under the impression he had frequent visitors. Unlike Evangeline, he wouldn't be throwing regular parties anytime soon.

"See who it is," the Grim Reaper commanded.

Xavier rose to his feet, and I hastened to join him—anything other than be left alone in the room with the Grim Reaper. When Xavier opened the door, it was to reveal the leader of the vampires herself, who strode into the hall as though she lived here.

"Is this a bad time?" Evangeline's gaze flickered in my direction.

What in the world was she doing here? Since when did she pay social calls to the Grim Reaper? I'd thought they hated one another.

"No, but I didn't know you had an appointment," said Xavier. "Boss, Evangeline is here."

"Is she?" said the Grim Reaper. "Send her in."

What? I stared, bemused, as she moved fluidly past me

and into the meeting room. When she settled in the chair I'd vacated, I looked past her at the Grim Reaper. "Weren't we in the middle of a meeting?"

"I think I've heard enough from you, Aurora," he responded. "You may take her home, apprentice."

Dismissed. Cursing the vampires' leader—and not shielding my thoughts—I left the house with Xavier at my side.

"Can you believe her?" I closed the door behind me. "I thought she hated your boss."

"So did I," he said. "Maybe she had the same idea as you did."

"Just great," I said. "I guess I won't get another shot at meeting with him anytime soon. Not that he seemed willing to listen to me anyway."

"Sorry about him." He glanced over his shoulder. "He doesn't understand people very well."

"Occupational hazard of being dead." I buried my hands in my pockets to stave off the chill. "I guess it doesn't matter to him if the paranormal world is exposed. I just wish I knew how to learn more about how and where the vampires are recruiting normals. Like, are they just showing up on the streets and ambushing random people, or what?"

More to the point, *who* was doing the recruiting? The Founders, or someone else?

He shot me a concerned look. "Vampires are hard to police, but if they're known to be crossing a line, it's usually up to the local vampire leader to pass judgement on them. Assuming there is one."

"I wouldn't know if there's a local vampire leader

where Laney lives," I said. "What with it being a normal town."

Given that the first vampires I'd ever seen had been Mortimer Vale and his friends and none of them had looked remotely like they belonged there, I had an inkling they weren't a common sight—or they hadn't been, before the Founders had zeroed in on my dad's old shop. It was hard for me not to imagine I might be the reason they'd picked that particular area as their recruiting ground.

Guilt churned within me, and I wrapped my arms around myself as we walked away from the cemetery and back towards the library. While it would have been nice to imagine Laney had become aware of the paranormal world via some innocent means, I couldn't discount the possibility that the vampires were looking for a new route to get to me. The leader of their little group was in jail, the library was warded against almost all threats, and my family were as prepared as possible to deal with the Founders if they showed their faces. We weren't helpless, not like I'd been when I'd been alone. But Laney, living an ordinary life without any idea of the dangers that had hounded me over the last three months, had been a prime target.

Xavier dropped me off outside the library, and we parted with a hug and kiss.

"Best of luck with your pointy-toothed friend," I said to him. "Say hi from me."

"I doubt she'll be interested in speaking to me," said Xavier. "It's my boss she wanted to talk to, and I can't say I know why."

"Maybe she'll tell you." I drew in a breath, taking out

my phone. "I'll see you soon, okay? I'm going to call Laney."

I opened the library door and walked in—then I halted, the door swinging shut behind me.

Aunt Adelaide and Estelle stood beside the front desk... and next to them was Laney.

10

Laney was here. *Here.* In my family's library.

"Laney." My jaw dropped. "What are you doing here?"

Please tell me she hadn't seen anything weird. Like someone using magic, or even a vampire walking around. Especially a vampire. *Oh, god. Why didn't I intervene sooner?*

Estelle met my eyes, which widened a fraction as though she wanted to ask me the same question. Which was impossible with my best friend standing in front of us. I couldn't exactly tell Laney that I'd just returned from an interview with the Grim Reaper in which we'd been interrupted by the leader of the local vampires.

"Um, this is Estelle," I said instead. "As you probably know. And that's my Aunt Adelaide."

Given that she wasn't panicking over the vampire in the basement, I'd guess she hadn't met Cass yet. Based on how Aunt Candace and Cass—the latter in particular— acted towards strangers, I'd be better off keeping her out of their way.

"I know," she said. "I just got here a minute ago. Sorry about the short notice, but I was in the area anyway, so I thought I'd drop by. You did say I could stay over, right? Just say the word and I'll leave. I don't want to bother you."

My mind helpfully went blank. "Oh. Good. I mean, you aren't bothering me, but I'm just surprised. Tell you what, want to come into my family's living quarters? It's warmer in there, and there's space for us to talk."

"Sure," she said. "I can't believe the size of this place. No wonder you fell head over heels right away. I know how much you love old books."

"Yeah." What must she think of us? Even on a non-workday, I still wore my long silver-lined cloak, embossed with my family's symbol—two crossed pens accompanied by an owl sitting on top of an open book. Not typical librarian attire. I surreptitiously removed my cloak and draped it over my shoulder as I traipsed behind Aunt Adelaide, past the stairs and into the living room.

The living quarters were fairly ordinary-looking by the library's standards—provided nobody opened the potion cabinet to reveal the jars of glittering pixie wings and other bizarre ingredients, that is. Oh, and as long as Sylvester didn't fly in. *Argh. What are we going to do when people start showing up looking for magical books?* Or if she went wandering around and ended up lost somewhere among the stacks? Even the most harmless books were distinctly magical. Sometimes they got into fights. Sometimes they bit people. And then there were places like the Dimensional Studies Section, the Magical Creatures Section, and the Vampire Section. I hadn't rehearsed for this. At all.

"Um, do you want anything to drink?" I asked her. "Tea, coffee… wine?"

Or a magical potion to make her forget? No, I'd already discarded that idea. Tricking my best friend didn't sit right with me, and besides, wiping her memory wouldn't help me figure out how she'd got here, nor how much of the magical world she'd seen already.

"Tea, if you have it," she said.

"I'll bring the drinks," Estelle offered, heading into the kitchen.

I knew she'd left us alone so I could talk to her in peace, but my mind remained blank with shock. Whenever I'd imagined introducing Laney to the library, it'd never looked like this, and the knowledge that someone other than me had told her this world existed made me feel off-balance for reasons I couldn't explain.

Only then did it hit me: I'd always planned to bring her into this world. I'd just hoped more than anything that her first experience with the magical world would be more pleasant than mine had been. That it wouldn't involve fearing for her life. Now someone had taken that decision away from her.

My throat closed up. "Laney, what happened to you?"

"What do you mean?" she asked. "What's wrong?"

"You…" I blinked the sting from my eyes. "You shouldn't have come. I know I should have told you sooner, but—this place isn't safe for you."

"Because it's magical?" she said. "Oh, please."

My mouth gaped open, but no words came out. Even the sound of Estelle making drinks in the kitchen sounded like it came from another planet.

She tilted her head. "You didn't think you could hide all this from me forever, did you?"

I swallowed my disbelief. "You knew? Since when?"

"Since... hmm. A while." She leaned forward in her seat. "I think part of me always knew there was something special about your family."

"You did?" I blinked, stupefied. "But how? You never met them."

"I was there, don't you remember?" she said. "At your dad's funeral. I saw your aunts hiding at the back, and I saw them leave early before you noticed."

"You *saw* them?" I gripped my knees with my hands. "You didn't tell me."

"I thought you'd met," she said. "I assumed you were on bad terms. Or they were distant relations. I don't know. But when you said they'd got in touch with you, I realised they must be the people I'd seen. So I went digging. It's amazing what you can find when you ask the right questions."

"To whom?" I said. "You... you told me you found it on the internet. Is that true?"

"I did," she said. "And my search led me here. Eventually. I hit a few dead ends, but I'm too persistent to give up that easily."

Shame flushed my chest. "I wanted to tell you. I always did. I was just... I was afraid someone would hurt you. Magic can be dangerous, especially to people who aren't prepared for it."

"Yeah, I know," she said. "I'm not going to run off, Rory."

My fingers dug into my knees again. "Also, there are rules about sharing this world with people from outside, and I didn't want to bring up the subject first in case it came back to hit me in some way. I mean, we're fairly isolated here on the coast, but that doesn't mean the rules don't apply. I worried they'd erase your memory or kick both of us out. And... and I wasn't sure you'd *want* to get involved."

"I knew you'd be looking out for me," she said, "Really, though, I'm fine. I mean, you have *magic.* How could I not want to get involved?"

"How much do you know, then?" I asked. "I mean, about the library? Because that's not information that should be floating around on the internet."

"I don't know much about the library, but I've read enough fantasy books to get the gist," she said. "You're a witch, so it stands to reason the library is magical, too."

Estelle walked back into the room with our drinks. I surreptitiously gave them a scan, but they appeared to be ordinary tea with a shot of a calming tonic. I probably needed it more than Laney did, so I took a huge sip.

"There's a lot to the magical world." I put down my teacup, relishing the calming sensation that flowed through my limbs. "More than witches and magic libraries, I mean. And the library itself is too complicated to explain without needing a few weeks. I'm still finding new things out every day."

"I'm capable of being patient, you know." She put down her teacup, her mouth tilting up at the corner. "I even gave you a few months to settle into your new life before I came barging in."

"Sorry," I said. "I'm trying to figure out where to start. My own introduction to the magical world wasn't exactly standard."

"I know," she said. "Your family got in touch after you got fired, right? Because you'd have had trouble keeping your flat and finding a new job if they hadn't intervened. And you heard about the library and couldn't say no. Even if it did involve moving in with a bunch of strangers."

That was a simple version of the story. Without the vampires. "Basically, yeah. I wouldn't have been able to afford rent if I hadn't taken the job, so I was backed into a corner when I moved here. I'm lucky we all got on so well."

"Your family seems really nice," she said. "They all look like you. Like your dad. I don't know why it didn't occur to me to ask if you had other family members. I remember that ghoul Abe exploiting you and nagging you about keeping your dad's old journal. Do you still have that?"

My mouth hung open for an instant. I'd forgotten I'd even mentioned the subject, but I must have told her about the journal back before I'd known it was anything special. "Yes, I do still have it, but Abe and I argued about everything. Believe me, I prefer working here to working at the bookshop, a thousand times over. With or without the magic."

"I bet," she said. "What's it like in here? Is it really as big as it looks on the outside?"

"Yes, but one of the corridors upstairs is invisible," I said. "My grandmother's the one who created the place, and she's the reason for all the weirdness."

Her eyes sparkled. "Invisible corridors? What else?"

I looked at the cloak I'd brought with me. "It's probably easier if I show you."

"You're going to use magic?" She sat up straighter,

while I pulled out my Biblio-Witch Inventory and displayed the pages. "Those are... words. *Find, travel...*"

I tapped the word *light,* and a ball of light appeared hovering above the book. Laney gaped at it. "The *words* are magical?"

"You've got it." I dispelled the light. "The words written in this book, that is. Each of my family members has the same kind of book. Our speciality is biblio-witch magic."

"Book witches." She bounced in her seat. "This is amazing, Rory. Show me another one."

"All right." I put down the Biblio-Witch Inventory and pulled out my wand. "This is for regular magic. Most witches and wizards have a wand. I'm still fairly new to mine—I got the biblio-witch magic first, because it runs in the family—but the wand used to be my dad's."

Her eyes rounded. "He lived here. Right?"

"He did." I gave a flick of my wand and levitated my Biblio-Witch Inventory into my hand. "And he left because my mum wasn't magical and there are rules against sharing this world with outsiders. After he died, I had no idea any of this existed until my aunts showed up, and the rest is history."

Her gaze followed the movement as I gave another wave of my wand, conjuring up a couple of books and then banishing them again. "Wow. A real magic wand. Your aunts and cousins are the same, right? Wait—what about that elusive boyfriend of yours?"

"He's busy," I evaded—I'd get to the *Grim Reaper* part later, when I was sure Evangeline was long gone. "But there's someone else I want you to meet."

"Oh?" She picked up one of the books, flicking through it. "Magical books, magical family…"

"And a magical familiar," I said. "Jet, come here."

The little crow zipped into view. "Here, partner!"

Laney jumped. "Oh, he's cute! He's your familiar? Does that mean you talk to one another?"

"We can, but that's because of an accident with a spell," I said. "Anyway, only my family and I can understand him."

"Handy." She reached out a hand and Jet landed on her palm, peering at her with curious eyes.

"Definitely," I said. "There's also a pixie, but he's new here and fairly shy. And an owl, but he's… not speaking to me at the moment. Best to just stick with Jet. He likes people. Jet, this is Laney."

Jet zipped around her head, chattering excitedly, while I finished off my tea and ran through a mental inventory of everything else that I wanted to show her. The bakery, the pier, the beach… and the rest of the library, of course.

Aunt Adelaide bustled into the room. "Dinner will be ready in an hour or so. Can I get you two anything else?"

"No, we're fine," I told her. "Is Cass around?"

"She's upstairs, of course," said Aunt Adelaide. "I wouldn't bother her. But I did rearrange things on the ground floor a little. It should be fine for you to have a look around, Laney. Just watch your step when climbing the stairs."

"Literally," I added to her. "The steps sometimes vanish, Hogwarts-style. Also, make sure you watch out for the owl. Have you seen Sylvester, Aunt Adelaide?"

"No, but I expect he's avoiding us, too," she said. "He doesn't like it when he's not the centre of attention."

Estelle bounded out of the kitchen to join us. "Want me to help?"

"Thanks," I said gratefully, figuring Laney and I would do better with a guide who could actually get the library to do what she wanted most of the time.

"We'll do the ground floor first," Estelle said. "As I told Rory when she first moved here, it would take literally days to see everything, especially on the upper levels. This way is the Reading Corner…"

Amazingly, the library cooperated for most of our tour. Laney was enamoured by the floating lanterns, and when I said they were lit by magic, I thought she was going to swoon on the spot. "Can I take one home? Joking, I know they're yours."

"More like the library's," said Estelle. "If you take anything out of the library, it can get a little… rowdy. Including the books, sometimes."

"I won't touch anything." Laney's gaze flickered across the shelves, landing on the translator box lying on the desk. "What's that?"

"Translator spell," I said. "For magical codes, that sort of thing."

While most of my apprehension had seeped away, it seemed like tempting fate to bring up the subject of my dad's journal again. I'd forgotten she even knew it existed, but of course, I hadn't known it was magical for the years I'd taken care of it. I'd just assumed Dad had lost the translator document, which wasn't that far out of character for him. I'd never have guessed that it might contain information that would put either of our lives in danger.

"I didn't know magic looked like this." She peered at the box. "Don't worry. I won't touch it."

"That spell should be safe as long as Aunt Candace hasn't left anything inside it," said Estelle. "Touching her notes is more hazardous than half the books, if possible."

Despite the library's many hazards, we finished our tour of the ground floor without anyone ending up at the mercy of Aunt Candace's pen. Soon after, Aunt Adelaide called us into the dining room.

Aunt Candace already sat at the end of the table, her notebook and pen at the ready, and an expectant look appeared on her face when Laney walked in. After the utter disaster she'd made of my one family dinner with Xavier, I was apprehensive at best at having her share a dinner table with my best friend.

"So this is the newcomer," said Aunt Candace. "It seems we're hosting normals in the library again."

"Why, have you had normals staying here before?" asked Laney.

Aunt Candace chuckled. "You've got the hang of our vocabulary fast, girl. Yes, we had an aspiring wizard who used to sleep in the Reading Corner. He went a bit mad, poor thing, and then he was murdered. Rory found the body, didn't you?"

I groaned. "Really, Aunt Candace?"

"Not at the dinner table," Aunt Adelaide said sternly. "Nobody is getting murdered, Laney."

"Exactly," said Estelle, with a significant look at Aunt Candace.

Seeing she was outnumbered, Aunt Candace shrugged and went back to eating. Cass never showed up at all, so she must still be hiding upstairs with the animals.

After dinner, I left Laney in the living room with

instructions not to touch anything and went looking for my missing cousin.

I didn't have to look hard. As soon as I went into the lobby, I nearly walked into Cass coming the other way, a book tucked underneath her arm.

"There you are," I said.

"If you're expecting me to come and introduce myself to our uninvited guest, forget it," she said. "Maybe she'll get the hint and go away."

"Excuse me?" I said. "You don't have to be unpleasant to her just because none of us expected her to show up. She's my best friend, but she's also a normal, which means we're her first experience of the paranormal world. Do you want to give her the impression that witches and wizards are rude and antisocial?"

"I don't trust her," said Cass.

"Because she's a normal?" I said. "She won't go around telling everyone about us."

"Yeah, like you weren't going to tell her," she said.

"I didn't tell her," I said. "She worked it out because we're best friends. It's not the same."

"Really?" she said. "Have you forgotten Maurice?"

My heart contracted. My dad's former best friend had wanted to be part of this world badly enough that he'd ended up committing murder for it. He'd been furious that my dad had been involved in the magical world without him, only to give it all up for my mother and me. Maurice's hatred had almost destroyed us, and I didn't blame Cass for not wanting a repeat experience.

But I didn't believe for a minute that Laney would make the same choice.

"Cass, Maurice was insecure and jealous," I said.

"Laney is neither of those things. She just doesn't want to lose touch with her best friend. Can you blame her?"

"This isn't her world," she insisted. "She doesn't belong here."

"Oh, thanks," said Laney from behind me. "I take it you're the cousin I haven't met yet?"

"This is Cass," I told her. "She doesn't like strangers."

"I gathered." Laney wrinkled her nose. "Why does she smell of sawdust?"

"She keeps pets," I explained. "She likes animals more than people, in fact."

Her eyes sparkled. "Magical pets? Do tell."

Cass snorted and walked off with her nose in the air. I, meanwhile, turned to Laney. "I don't know what she's keeping upstairs at the moment and I'm not sure I want to know, to be honest."

"I do," she said. "I want to know it all. Nothing is too outrageous for me."

Despite everything, I grinned. The magical world hadn't frightened her off, and I could finally bring her into my new life without worrying she'd be scared away from me for good.

Sure, we'd have some trouble along the way, but the hard part was done, and no matter what else happened, we'd be able to face it together.

11

We reached the morning without any major disasters happening. The library seemed to understand that Laney was a guest, because it didn't trap her in the corridor or rearrange the staircases the way it'd done to me when I'd first moved here. I could only assume Aunt Adelaide had had stern words with Cass and Sylvester, too.

"I slept like a log," Laney announced, appearing in the doorway of the guest room when I knocked.

I'm glad Sylvester didn't wake you up. He'd left feathers in my bed at some point, but he hadn't disturbed me during the night.

"Good," I said. "Want to head to Zee's bakery and grab breakfast?"

Visiting Zee turned out to be a good move. Laney grew even more excited when I told her that her normal-world currency would work just fine here. She left the bakery laden with three bags of goodies, and then insisted on walking up the high street and then around the square to look at all the shops. I practically had to drag her away from the pet shop, where she was entranced by the various birds and cats and other magical animals.

"Oh, hey," said Alice, the friendly witch who ran the pet store. "Are you new in town?"

"I am," said Laney. "Ooh, I like that snake. Python, right?"

Alice smiled, petting the snake which coiled around her shoulders. "He is. He likes you."

"He does?" Her eyes sparkled, and she reached out to pet the snake. I, meanwhile, had to fend off an overzealous snowy owl who wanted to make a nest in my hair. I already had a familiar, and besides, I could just see how Sylvester would react to another owl being present in the library.

"You're as bad as Cass," I whispered to Laney. "You can't buy a magical hawk and take it back with you into the normal world. What would people think?"

"I never really cared what the normals think," she said.

No wonder she'd been so quick to adapt to the magical world—though it helped that most vampires didn't frequent the local shops. They tended to stick to their creepy old houses and graveyards.

"C'mon." I tugged on her arm as she leaned longingly towards the hawk. "Want to see the beach?"

"Yes, please." Predictably, that got her attention, and she forgot all about the pet shop in favour of running up to the pier to look at the sea. The cool breeze brought the scent of sea-salt and tangled my hair.

"I bet this place is gorgeous in summer," she said.

"Yeah, I didn't pick the best time of year to move to the

seaside." I spotted a glittering mane out at sea. "Hey… I think that's Cass's kelpie out there."

I waved to the water horse, who raised his head in greeting and then plunged beneath the water again. I didn't think Laney would pull an Aunt Candace and try riding him, but the kelpie had made a wise move to stay away from the shore to avoid taking a human passenger for an unplanned swim.

After we'd enjoyed the view for a bit, we retraced our path to the library so I could show Laney some of the other floors.

"So, is this your official job now?" she asked. "Is it basically the same as a regular library, with added magic?"

"Usually," I said. "Aunt Adelaide runs things behind the scenes, Estelle's in charge of hospitality, and the rest of us handle the books. Which usually translates to the three of us doing most of the work while Cass hangs out with her animals and Aunt Candace works on her latest manuscript."

Cass was being her usual antisocial self, while there was still no sign of Sylvester. Laney and I were better off that way, but a teetering pile of returns lay in the box beside the front desk. When I picked one up, the stack fell over, sending books scattering all over the reception area.

"Ack." I cringed when Laney made to pick up one of the books and it snapped its pages at her. "I wouldn't pick them up. Jet, I need your help."

"Hello, partner!" The little crow flew down to meet me.

"Can you make sure nothing disturbs Laney while I sort these out?" I asked him. "Laney, give me a shout if you need me, okay?"

"I don't need a babysitter, you know," she said. "I'll head to the Reading Corner. There's a new sci-fi book I like the look of."

I opened my mouth to ask her if it was one of Aunt Candace's, and a cool blast of air hit me from behind. I rose to my feet to find Evangeline had entered soundlessly, her brows rising at the sight of the books scattered on the floor.

Why? Why Now?

"Evangeline," I said, trying to keep the panic from my voice. "Can I help you?"

"Aurora," she said. "Did my eyes deceive me, or were you meeting with the Grim Reaper yesterday?"

"I was." No point in denying it. *Um, you know we're not open on Sundays, don't you?*

She made no response to my thoughts, though her gaze followed Laney's path towards the Reading Corner. As a human, Laney's mind would be wide open.

"Everything is still going well with his apprentice, then?" she asked.

"Of course." Had she really come here expecting me to answer a Q&A on my relationship with Xavier?

"I'm glad to hear it," she said. "I notice the two of you didn't come to my party together."

Okay, why was she so interested in my boyfriend? "I didn't think you two were friends. Anyway, it was my aunt who got us the invitations."

"Yes, she wanted to speak to Lord Vogel about his life in the 19th Century," she said. "Was it productive for her?"

"I think it was. You'll have to ask her." Why in the world was the leader of the vampires making small talk with me? "She got a lot of useful information, before…"

"Before the unfortunate incident with one of my guests." Annoyance spiked in her voice. "Whoever was responsible remains as elusive as ever."

"Oh." If she was talking openly about the murders, she wouldn't object to me asking a question or two, right? "I actually have something related I want to ask you."

A flicker of some unreadable expression passed through her eyes. "What is it?"

"Normals." I swallowed against my dry throat. "I heard… from some of the guests at the party that a vampire in the area is recruiting normals to join them. I don't know who to report it to, as they're from a town which doesn't have a local head vampire."

"Were they present at the party?" she asked. "Did these humans seem distressed in any way, or suffering any signs of vampiric interference?"

Vampiric interference. Meaning, side-effects from drinking their blood or from being bitten.

"No," I replied. "They… they seemed normal. They also seemed to think the vampires wouldn't harm them."

"There you have it," she said. "If the normals walked into our world with their eyes wide open, there's nothing I or any of the others could possibly have done to stop them. It's hardly an uncommon occurrence."

"Really?" I said. "What if the vampires in question are part of a certain group known for stirring up trouble?"

Her gaze focused on me, and the air seemed to tighten in response. "Do you have proof of this?"

I shook my head. "I know the Founders were in the area, and two normals I overheard talking were recruited from a place I know the Founders are familiar with.

Maybe the vampire they work for knows who was responsible for the murders."

"An interesting theory," she said, "but until I see some proof of the identity of these so-called *vampire recruiters,* it's not worth abandoning my people for a pointless quest."

Typical. I should have guessed that Evangeline wouldn't care about normals being recruited by her fellow vampires unless she was directly affected herself. Even the victims hadn't been friends of hers. Not the first one, anyway. As for the second—

Her expression shifted, and my heart gave another lurch. I'd forgotten to shield my thoughts.

"The vampire in question was an unpleasant individual who won't be missed," she said. "Does that assuage your fears that your family might become targets?"

My mouth parted. "It's not just my family I'm worried about. Um, was there a book you wanted to take out? Or return?"

Her gaze went to my shoulder bag, where I always kept my spare notebook… and my dad's journal. Then she gave a pointed look at the Reading Corner, where she'd doubtless seen Laney walking. A rush of protectiveness swept through me.

"I merely wished to check you were safe, given the attempted break-in the night of the party."

How on earth had she known someone had tried to break into the library? My aunts hadn't reported it to the police. Annoyance replaced my protective impulse, and I fixed on a false smile. "We're fine, thanks for asking. I don't mean to be rude, but my aunt will want me to remind you that we're closed for the weekend."

"Of course." She gave me a false smile that illuminated her inhumanly beautiful face. "I won't disturb you any longer."

She disappeared, the door closing softly behind her. I released a slow breath, then ducked to the floor to collect the returns I'd dropped.

"Just checking up on me, was she?" I muttered. "A likely story."

Laney popped up from behind a shelf. "What's going on?"

"Nothing." I'd been more than happy to introduce her to the magical world, but the vampire murders, the group hunting for my dad's journal... those weren't things I wanted her mixed up in. Not at all. "That was Evangeline, head of the local vampires. You know what I said about the magical world being dangerous? About ninety percent of it applies to her and her friends."

"Vampires are real, too," she said, in thoughtful tones. "I didn't see any when we were out earlier. Are there werewolves, too?"

She was still wrapped up in her fascination over the magical world, but would that last when she saw its darker side? I'd been living in Ivory Beach for weeks before I'd met Evangeline for the first time and she'd still scared me half to death.

"Sure," I said. "There's also a wererabbit who runs the local flower shop and an elf in charge of the police force, but they won't take kindly to you gawking at them."

"I'll behave," she said. "I'm more interested in seeing the library for now. And that elusive boyfriend of yours, now we can talk about all this openly."

"Ah, I haven't heard from him today," I said. "My

phone signal's acting up again, as you probably gathered from my messages. For some reason, the library scrambles the phone signals and internet connection."

"Probably all the magic." She grinned. "Is he a wizard, anyway? You never said."

It couldn't hurt at this point. "He's a Reaper."

Her jaw hit the floor. "You mean, the type who carries a scythe and steals people's souls?"

"He doesn't steal souls, he takes them into the afterlife," I said. "But yes, essentially."

She whistled. "He wasn't carrying a scythe. Though it explains why he wears so much black."

"His scythe is always there, it just turns invisible when he doesn't want it on display," I said. "He's technically the Grim Reaper's apprentice… who you definitely *don't* want to meet. His boss makes the vampires look cuddly and pleasant."

She laughed. "Now, that's an endorsement."

"Everything okay?" Estelle approached us from the stacks. "Oh—wow, that's a lot of returns."

"Sorry, I knocked them over." I put two of the books back into place. "And then Evangeline interrupted me."

"What did she want?" She waved her wand and returned several of the books to their box. "She knows we're not open, right?"

"She claims to be concerned for our well-being after our narrow escape the other night." I stacked the remaining books back on the desk. "Not sure what brought that on. I was worried I might have to bring Aunt Adelaide in to drive her off, considering we're supposed to be closed to the public."

"Huh." She picked up one of the returns. "First floor… want me to handle these?"

"I'll help," I said. "Tell you what, Laney, you can come with us to help with the returns. Just keep your distance from the books that bite."

With two of us watching, I was less concerned about her potentially falling victim to a trap. While Estelle and I gathered the relevant books, the pixie flitted above Laney's head, but judging by the way she didn't glance up and stare at him, he'd glamoured himself invisible to her as he usually did when he was around strangers.

When we reached the first floor, I spotted an elusive feathered shape sitting on a shelf. The owl turned away when he saw me looking, but Laney spotted him instantly.

"Oh." She pointed. "Is that owl supposed to be up there?"

Sylvester ignored me and instead addressed Laney. "And who might you be?"

"I'm Laney," she replied. "You're the other familiar, right? Sylvester?"

"The one and only." He fluffed his feathers. "Have the humans told you everything about me?"

"Hm." She glanced at me. "Rory said you were an owl familiar who talks, but you're not talking to her right now for some reason."

"Because I accidentally hit him with a spell," I said. "Not on purpose. I said I was sorry a dozen times."

"Did she tell you that I practically run the library myself?" the owl said.

"He's in charge of late fees," I explained. "And Aunt Adelaide does most of the admin. He probably does Aunt Candace's share, though."

"I am worth ten of her," said the owl.

"Of course you are." It was probably best to play along in case he decided to punish both of us by setting the book wraith loose from the Vampire Section or something. "You're the best owl in the library."

Laney gave me a look that asked *isn't he the only owl in the library,* but thankfully she didn't say anything aloud to provoke his ire.

Sylvester swooped around flinging useless advice at us while we returned the books to their correct places, but refrained from doing anything to frighten Laney. Perhaps he wanted to make a good impression on her, or at least not scare her into leaving the library and never coming back. The time slid by, and it came as a surprise when Aunt Adelaide called us downstairs to tell us it was getting late.

"Rory, it's almost dark outside," she said. "If your friend wants to go home, it's probably better if you head back before the sun goes down."

"Fair point," I said. "Laney, what do you think?"

"Oh, sure," she said. "Do you have a broomstick lying around, or...?"

"I can do a transportation spell," I told her. "It's a pretty simple one. I'll tap on a word in my Biblio-Witch Inventory, and we'll be home in a second."

"Travel by biblio-witch magic? I like it."

"It's handy," I said. "You should go and pack up your stuff. I'll wait down here."

Laney headed upstairs to her guest room, and I said to Aunt Adelaide, "Sorry she showed up unannounced."

"Don't apologise, Rory," she said. "I know how hard it is to maintain friendships outside of the magical community. I'm glad she adapted to the library so readily."

"Yeah." I drew in a breath. "Is there a way I can help her stay safe while I'm not around? "Specifically, from vampires? Evangeline doesn't seem concerned about the Founders going after normals, and I'd sleep a lot easier if I knew she was safe from being recruited."

"I had an inkling the issue might come up, so I prepared this." She reached into her pocket and handed me a pendant inset with a silver jewel. "This protective charm will keep her safe, provided she keeps hold of it. No vampires can touch her while she's wearing it."

"Thanks," I said, with a rush of gratitude. "I'll give it to her."

I met Laney at the foot of the stairs, handing her the pendant. She took it, her brow creasing in puzzlement.

"What's this?" she asked.

"It's to protect you against danger from the magical world," I said. "Can you promise me you'll keep it on you at all times, especially when you leave the house?"

Vampires required an invitation to enter someone's home, and Laney had enough common sense not to let one of them into her house. But I still didn't trust them an inch.

She slipped the pendant into her pocket, while I took out my Biblio-Witch Inventory ready to return us home. On impulse, I dropped my bag onto the front desk so Dad's journal would be safely stowed in the library while I took her back, in case the vampires were waiting on the other side.

Laney caught up to me at the desk. "I had a great time. Thank you for letting me stay."

"Anytime." I held up my Biblio-Witch Inventory and moved my finger down the page, in search of the right word. "Stand closer to me... I should be able to take us both at the same time." It'd worked with Xavier, after all.

"Hmm." She gave the library one last scan as though trying to commit every detail to memory.

Then I hit *travel,* and we were off. The library blurred around us, Laney staggered against the desk and I caught her arm to make sure she wasn't left behind—and a second later, we landed next to the river. No matter how I tried, I couldn't seem to stop myself from transporting both of us to that same road, but at least I hadn't landed in the water.

Laney caught her balance faster than I did. "Is that quicker than flying on a broom?"

"I haven't even learned to fly on a broomstick yet," I said. "But yeah, it's definitely more efficient. Want me to walk you home, or are you okay to go from here?"

"I'll be fine." She hugged me goodbye. "I'll be back before you know it."

Then she was gone, walking down the high street and out of sight. I watched her go, my insides churning with a mixture of emotions. Happiness at seeing her, guilt at keeping the magical world a secret from her for so long, worry about leaving her alone, apprehension, and a whole lot more. The part of me which was keen to invite her back warred with the knowledge that every visit to the paranormal world would make it harder for her to leave. As long as she kept the pendant close at hand, she ought to be safe from vampires, at least... but that didn't mean my worries would go away as easily.

A flickering movement stirred in the corner of my eye.

I turned around, my shoulders stiffening at the sight of a tall figure on the bridge, the light of a streetlamp making his shadow stretch behind him.

I knew him, this time. There was no doubt. He was one of Mortimer Vale's companions. When he caught my eye, he smiled, recognising me, too.

Heart thumping, I approached the bridge. "What are you doing here?"

"Looking for someone who can help us find what we are searching for, of course," said the vampire in a high, cold voice.

Movement flickered behind my shoulder, and another figure stepped lithely into view. Shorter than the first vampire but no less scary, he wore a black hat atop his slick dark hair.

"I won't give you the journal," I told them.

"Sweetheart, we don't need it," said the second vampire in a low, raspy voice. "It's worthless without a translation."

"Then why are you still stalking me?" I reached in my pocket for the firedust, my hands shaking. Then I flung it to the ground at my feet.

Flames sparked from the dust, sparks flying into their faces. The two vampires recoiled with inhuman speed, hissing with anger, then fled into the darkening streets.

I sucked in a quick breath, then two. Laney had the protective charm. She was safe, in theory, from being pursued by those vampires. But that didn't mean they'd give up chasing me. I had to warn my family.

I used my Biblio-Witch Inventory to transport myself back home, reeling on the spot when I landed in the lobby.

"Whoa," said Estelle. "Rough journey?"

"Vampires," I said. "Mortimer Vale's two friends. They cornered me when I was alone."

Maybe I'd been their intended target… or maybe they'd been after Laney, but they'd been unable to get near her as long as she was carrying the protective charm.

Estelle hurried to my side. "Breathe, Rory."

"I threw firedust at them and chased them off." I inhaled and exhaled, willing my heart to stop racing. "They were waiting for me, I'm sure."

Or Laney.

"Rory?" Aunt Adelaide approached us. "You took your friend home?"

"And ran into some vampires," I said. "Mortimer Vale's two buddies were waiting there on the bridge as though they belonged there."

Why had they been there? If they were recruiting people, there were more efficient ways to go about it than hanging around on a bridge when most people had gone home.

Whatever the case, I could think of only one way to get answers about what the two of them were up to without throwing my friends and family in the line of fire: I had to speak to Mortimer Vale again.

12

"Absolutely not," Edwin said. "This is a jail, not a place to mingle and socialise. Besides, we're closed to visitors."

I'd expected him to say no, not least because it was still Sunday night, but I hadn't the time to wait for my message to Laney to go through. I needed answers, now.

"Edwin, I wouldn't ask if it wasn't really important," I said. "I just ran into Mortimer Vale's two friends in the normal town where I used to live. I think they're hassling my best friend, and I need to know if he put them up to it."

His mouth thinned. "I'm responsible for policing this region, not the towns outside of the magical community. I can't do anything about these vampires. If they're threatening your friends, might I suggest asking Evangeline instead?"

"She won't help either," I said quietly. "I already mentioned it to her, but she's unconcerned with anything that happens outside of Ivory Beach. I'm not asking you to send anyone after the pair of them, but it's possible they'll show up here next, and I bet Mortimer Vale knows what they're planning."

"And will he tell you the truth, or will he give you a pile of useless riddles to make you doubt yourself again?" he said. "There is categorically no way for him to know what his friends are up to, because nobody who has visited him during his time in jail has set eyes on them."

"Except for me," I added. "And if he reads my thoughts, he can draw his own conclusions. Like about the death at Evangeline's party, for instance. He might be able to tell me who did it by reading the details from my mind."

"And what makes you think he'll be honest with you?" he said.

"He isn't friendly with the killer, whoever it is," I said. "And I'm sure he wouldn't object to them being put behind bars."

I hoped so, anyway. After my terrifying run-in with those vamps yesterday, the last thing I wanted was to end up in an enclosed space with one of them again, especially one who excelled at mental manipulation. But it was that or risk them going after Laney again.

Aunt Adelaide and Estelle were on my side, while Aunt Candace had dropped not-so-subtle hints that she'd be more than happy to come with me to the jail, too. I'd figured Edwin was even less likely to say yes if I had Aunt Candace with me along with her notebook and pen, so I'd turned down her offer.

Edwin sighed. "All right, but I won't have my guards bring him out of his cell, not like last time. If you want to talk to him, you'll need to go into the jail yourself. He's in an isolated area, so there won't be any danger of the other prisoners getting ideas. We had to isolate him because he kept scaring everyone in the vicinity by repeating their private thoughts back at them."

Typical vampire. "Thanks, Edwin. I'll let you know if I find out anything useful."

I waited while he went to exchange a few words with his two troll guards, sending one of them through the back door of the police station into the corridor leading to the prison cells. The second troll beckoned to me to follow him.

"Thanks," I whispered to the troll guard. "I'm doing this for the safety of everyone in town. I swear I'm not trying to annoy you."

"I hope it's worth speaking to him," rumbled the troll. "He keeps muttering about you. It's creepy."

I suppressed a shiver. "I bet."

Through the back doors, a short corridor led into the prison itself. I walked past a row of barred holding cells and came to an abrupt halt. Mortimer Vale sat on a wooden bench behind a glass wall, his eyes flickering in my direction.

"It's reinforced with spells," the troll said to me. "He kept breaking the bars off the regular cells, so this was the only vampire-proofed solution we could find."

Mortimer Vale regarded me with an expectant look on his face as I approached his glass-walled cell.

"Aurora," he said. "If I didn't know better, I'd say you enjoy my company."

"Don't flatter yourself." I positioned myself against the back wall, as far from the vampire as possible.

"I assume there's a good reason you're here, then," he said, his gaze flickering to the troll guards behind me.

"I saw two of your friends making trouble in a non-magical community," I told him. "They tried to corner me."

"Was that when you were returning your little human companion to her proper place?"

"Keep her out of this," I said.

A smile tugged at his mouth. "Are you going to ask me how I heard about her?"

"By reading my thoughts, how else?" As per usual, I was starting to regret ever coming to talk to him. I should have known he'd use Laney in an attempt to distract me.

"If that's what you'd prefer to believe," he said.

"Look, two of your people *threatened* me," I told him. "They've been hanging around and recruiting normals to join them, haven't they? They want my dad's journal, and they're prepared to lie and threaten ordinary humans to get what they want."

"Your point?" He didn't even try to deny my words, and his expectant expression remained intact.

I glared at him. "I know one of your people was responsible for the two vampire murders. I also know they're evading the law by hiding among normals. What do you say to *that?*"

"You're mistaken," he said. "My former companions desire the journal, that's all. They're not interested in leaving a trail of bodies behind them. However, that's not to say all my fellow searchers have any qualms about ensuring nobody else gets hold of the journal, by any means possible. It is highly valued, of course."

Who does he mean? Anyone who wasn't part of his small contingent, which might be any vampire at all.

"Murderers or not, your friends are hanging out

somewhere they have no business being in," I told him. "They're on the brink of violating the magical laws."

"I have no contact with the pair of them," he said. "Perhaps you should try asking your friend instead of me."

"Laney has nothing to do with your people." And I'd prefer to keep it that way.

"I really don't think you're going to get the answers you need if you insist on ignoring the truth, Aurora."

My throat went dry. "You're admitting to sending your people after my best friend?"

"I didn't give them the orders, no," he said. "And it might not have been one of them who got to her. Frankly, I believe it was noble of her to conceal the truth from you, and even more of her to come here and act as though nothing was wrong in order to set your mind at ease."

A hand clenched over my heart. "You're lying."

He must be. Yet Laney lived right in the vampires' recruitment ground, and she hadn't reacted as I'd expected to the magical world at all. Sure, she had an explanation, but Mortimer Vale's poisonous words knocked me off-balance.

Anger sparked inside me. How dare he make me doubt my best friend?

"I'm only telling the truth as I see it, Aurora," he said. "I witnessed you leave your old life behind without any cares whatsoever, so it wasn't hard to guess that you'd leave your former friends vulnerable to the magical world. If I were free to give my allies instructions, I might have told them to act in a different way, but it's too late now."

Too late. "You have no idea what you're talking about.

You haven't left the jail. You can't even read the other prisoners' minds. Unless you've had more visitors?"

"If you're referring to Evangeline, she came here to gloat at me the other day," he said casually. "She even tried to blackmail me, if you can believe it. She wanted to know if my two companions were responsible for the recent deaths. Naturally, I set her right on that one."

Evangeline had talked to him? That must be how she found out about my previous visit to the jail. "Did you tell *her* your buddies are targeting normals?"

"Don't be ridiculous," he said. "I told Evangeline the truth: I have no contact with my fellow vampires. I know only what I can infer from scanning the minds of others, but I have enough experience to know the signs which indicate a person is in a vampire's thrall. With your friend, those signs are as clear as night."

I backed up against the wall, the cold stone sending a chill through the fabric of my cloak. *In a vampire's thrall.* Like the book had said. "It's also clear that you get a kick out of winding me up. How can I believe a word you say?"

He smiled. "You wouldn't need to doubt, if you hadn't resisted me. If you hadn't run."

"You *threatened* me," I said. "You tried to steal my property, when I didn't even know about the paranormal world at all. Even back then, I would never have done as you asked."

"So you do carry more fire in you than I thought," he mused. "I'm pleased my companions' fixation on you wasn't a wasted effort."

Fire. The image of those two vampires fleeing from my flames came to mind and I focused on it, certain that he was probing my thoughts. Sure enough, his eyes narrowed.

"Brave, but not enough," he said softly. "Not enough to confront your friend. If I were you, I'd want to know what they did to her. Did you know that when a human is under a vampire's command, they can be asked to do things that they would never normally do? Evangeline took that risk when she invited normals to her party, but it is you who invited one of them into your home."

"Liar." The word rang hollow, and the buzz of my phone nearly made me jump out of my skin. Laney, texting me back to let me know she'd arrived home safe. Since the message had been sent hours ago, that wasn't enough of a reassurance to put my fears at bay. Especially after the bombshell Mortimer Vale dropped on me.

I sucked in a quick breath. *All right.* If I had to, I'd call Laney here and now and make sure she was safe and as far away from those vampires as possible.

I turned my back on the vampire's cell and walked down the corridor and out of earshot before I called her. Laney picked up right away.

"Rory?" she said. "Hey. What's up?"

"I…" I didn't want to do this. I didn't want to believe Mortimer Vale over her. I only wanted the truth. "I ran into two vampires just after you left. You didn't see them, did you?"

"Vampires." She swore under her breath. "Which vampires?"

"Laney." I closed my eyes. "If you're in trouble, you can tell me, you know that, right? If the vampires are threatening or manipulating you, my family and I can help you. But only if you tell me."

"Okay," she said. "Um, I'll level with you. It was a weird experience, and I didn't know how much to tell you."

"Go on." I tried to keep my words calm, measured.

"So, two strangers came to talk to me when I was on my way back from work the other week," she began.

My heart gave a sickening dive. "Did they dress like they'd walked out of a Victorian novel, by any chance?"

"You've got it," she said. "They said they wanted to get in touch with you, but they couldn't get hold of you. They also mentioned you promised to give them the journal that belonged to your dad. Obviously, I told them I had no idea where it was, but they seemed to think there was some kind of translation document in Abe's old shop."

My throat went dry. "They what?"

"Yeah, weird, huh?" she said. "I take it they already asked you, and you said no?"

"They did," I said. "But are you okay? I mean, they didn't hurt or threaten you?"

"They didn't… bite me or anything, if that's what you mean," she said. "You know I'm furious that they targeted you, too, right? I was hopping mad when I found out they'd been threatening you for months. No wonder you moved away. Anyway, the rest of it—seeing your relatives at the funeral and putting two and two together about where you'd moved to—that was the truth, Rory. I just wasn't sure how to tell you the rest."

I gripped the phone hard. "I believe you, but… are you sure they didn't try to coerce you into joining them? Mortimer Vale—he's their leader—seems to think they did."

"Mortimer Vale?" she said. "Sounds like a serial killer's name. I think I'd know if I met someone like that."

"You didn't, because he's in jail for trying to murder me," I said. "During my first week in town. I didn't mention that part earlier because I was trying not to freak you out."

I quickly told her about my first encounter with the three vampires in Abe's shop, and my family's subsequent rescue mission.

"Those evil little worms," she said. "I knew right off that those two were seriously shady. It wouldn't surprise me if they were still poking around Abe's shop."

"They're not," I said. "I mean, they knew the journal wasn't there, and there's no translation—my dad never had one. But that doesn't mean I'll let them get away with threatening you."

"It's fine," she said. "I didn't see anyone on my walk home, and I'm safe now I'm at my house. Vampires can't get in without being invited. That's what I heard."

"It's true," I said, "but you should still be careful in case they come after you anyway. They're persistent, and... and two vampires were murdered in the region in the last week. Did you know?"

"No wonder you were so freaked out," she said. "No, I didn't hear about them. You take care of that family of yours, right, Rory?"

"I will, but please, can you tell me if you see any vampires at all?" I asked. "Our local vampire leader won't take responsibility for any crimes committed by vampires outside of Ivory Beach, but that doesn't make it any less of a crime that they're recruiting humans and threatening people."

"I'll tell you if I see anything," she said. "I'll see you soon, okay?"

The call ended. For a moment, I stared at the phone, my heart thudding. *Damn you, vampires.* I should have known they wouldn't have given up after Mortimer Vale's arrest. Not only had they gone after Laney, they'd probably gone after my former boss, too. Abe wasn't a nice person, but that didn't mean he deserved to be tormented by a bunch of cranky immortals. *There's no translator document in the shop. I'd have known if there was.*

Drawing in a deep breath, I walked back to Mortimer Vale's cell.

He gave me a smile. "She's still lying to you."

"Shut up," I said, incensed. "You don't know a thing about us. Besides, you can't read someone's mind over the phone."

"No, but it's obvious she's had more than a single conversation with my companions," he said. "I wonder which vampire she's working for. They all want the journal, and if they told her where it was… perhaps that's why she came to the library. She knew you'd let her in, even uninvited."

"She'd rather eat dirt than help your two friends," I shot at him. "Or go near the people who threatened me or my family. If I have to put them behind bars myself, I will."

"I look forward to it," he said.

I couldn't stand being next to his smug face for a moment longer. I left the jail, blinking back tears, wanting to see Laney so much it hurt. I hadn't been able to stop the vampires from barging into her life after all. If I hadn't given her the protective charm, they might well have got her again as soon as I'd taken her home. Like they'd nearly got to me.

Wait. I hadn't picked up my bag after my return, nor had I checked on the journal. It ought to be where I left it, but the memory of Mortimer Vale's taunts sent a wave of panic washing over me. I half-ran back towards the square and across to the library.

"Rory!" Alice called after me from outside the pet shop. "Is your friend gone?"

I caught my breath. "She went home, yes."

I hope she's okay. I hope she's safe. I opened my mouth to find a polite way to say goodbye to Alice, but she added, "I wondered if she was staying in town when I saw her the other night."

"The other night?" I echoed.

"Yeah, the night everyone went to that party at Evangeline's place," she said. "I saw her hanging around the library."

The library. At the time of the attempted break-in.

No way.

But Alice had no idea about our conflict with the vampires. She had no reason to lie.

Alice called after me, but I was already heading back to the library. When I reached the doors, I slammed inside and ran straight to the desk, startling Sylvester into flight.

"What *are* you doing, you clumsy spatula?" he said. "You just took five hundred years off my life."

"You just made that up." I ran around the desk, heedless of the owl's protests. "Where's my bag? The one I left behind when I went to take Laney home?"

"How should I know? I'm too busy watching to make sure you don't invite a tarantula shifter into the library next."

"That sounds more like Cass than me." I crouched

down, finding my bag lying under the desk, its contents strewn over the floor. "Who knocked this over? When did you get here?"

"I've been here since you left, you ungrateful conch shell," he said.

"Your insults are getting weirder." I got down on hands and knees, searching everywhere, but the sinking feeling in the pit of my stomach was impossible to ignore.

No matter how hard I looked, I couldn't find it. The journal had gone.

13

I turned, ready to leave the library with the intention of returning to the jail, but of course, Mortimer Vale couldn't have been the one to steal it. Neither had his two friends, considering they'd appeared in front of me less than a minute after I'd left the library.

No, I'd left the journal here, and the instant I'd turned my back, someone had taken it.

There was a knock on the door. I marched over with my wand at the ready and yanked it open.

"Whoa, Rory," Xavier said. "Your family said you went to the jail again—"

"I did, and they got Laney." I lowered my wand. "I mean, she already met the vampires. Mortimer Vale's friends tried to recruit her weeks ago. I didn't want to believe it, but I called her just then and she told me a totally different version of her story to the one she told me when she came here. On top of that, my dad's journal is missing."

And that wasn't even getting into what Alice had just told me.

"Whoa." Xavier's brows shot up. "Slow down, Rory. Where did the journal go missing? When?"

"I left it here." I circled the desk and picked up my bag. "When I took Laney back. I don't know when it disappeared. I came back an hour or so ago, but I went to the jail immediately afterwards. Sylvester has been here since I left, right?"

Unless *he'd* taken the journal as yet another form of revenge on me for that freeze-frame spell.

"Yes, I have," he informed me. "Since that delightful vampire queen keeps inviting herself inside without permission, I've been appointed to watch the doors."

There was one way to figure this one out. "Jet, are you here?"

"Partner!" Jet flitted over to me.

"Is Sylvester telling the truth?" I asked, ignoring his huff of annoyance. "Was he watching the door the whole time? Did you see anyone knock my bag off the desk and take my journal?"

"No, partner!" he squeaked. "I didn't see anyone take it."

"Rory?" Estelle walked out of the living quarters, drawn by the noise. "Oh, hey, Xavier. What's going on?"

I drew in a breath. "My journal's missing. I left my bag behind in case the vampires showed up when I took Laney back, but... have you seen it?"

"No." Her eyes widened. "I didn't know you left it behind."

"I should have told you, but it was a last-minute impulse," I said. "When I got back here after those vampires attacked me, my first instinct was to go back to see if Mortimer Vale knew what his two buddies were playing at. I know *they* weren't here, but someone must have come in and taken it."

"They didn't," Estelle said. "Spark has been watching the door ever since you went to take Laney back, haven't you?"

The pixie appeared in a shower of glitter. Sylvester clucked his beak disapprovingly as Spark spoke to Estelle in a low voice.

Estelle gave Sylvester a stern look. "He says you did knock the bag off the desk."

"Tattle-tale," muttered the owl.

"But he didn't see anyone take the journal either," she added.

"That's impossible," I said. "I dropped it on the desk right before I activated the spell to take Laney back."

Estelle crouched down to help me search. "I wish I'd stayed with you. I didn't think—but are you sure it's not just Mortimer Vale playing mind games?"

"Believe me, I want to believe it is."

"He's lying," said Xavier. "You trust Laney, don't you? More than you should trust Mortimer Vale."

"I do," I said, "but she didn't tell me the vampires had already tried to recruit her and didn't give me the full picture of how she discovered the magical world, either. I know I skipped over a few things as well, but I was trying to protect her."

"Maybe she thought the same," he said. "I don't know her well enough to make excuses for her, but I'd believe almost anyone over that Mortimer Vale and his ilk. Did they really try to chase you earlier?"

"They did, but I threw firedust at them."

"Good," he said, with more vehemence than I'd usually expect from him. "I'm glad, Rory. I should have been there —I didn't know your friend would be paying a visit on such short notice."

"Nor did I, which should have been my biggest clue," I said. "She showed up on the doorstep while I was out meeting with your boss. I couldn't exactly kick her out, but she took the magical world in stride. I should have known there was something odd about how quickly she accepted everything."

My throat tightened, thinking of how thrilled she'd been to meet my family and to explore the library. It couldn't have all been a trick. No way.

"She might not have been faking," said Xavier. "I didn't think she seemed duplicitous in the slightest when we met."

"No, well, she didn't know what *you* were until I told her," I said. "And I didn't think she knew everything about me, either. She just knew I was magical. But the vampires told her things. And you know how manipulative they are."

Especially when I'd left her wide open to being recruited by vampires in my absence. I should have known they would stop at nothing to get the journal from me.

I shouldn't have left her behind. I should have known the magical world would catch up to her anyway.

"I believe you, but she said they didn't bite her, right?" he said. "She's not under their control."

"Biting isn't the only way for a vampire to make a

human obey them." I blinked hard. "My journal is missing again, and she was the last person to see it."

What if the worst had happened and the vampires had told Laney to steal it for them? I felt like the worst friend in the world for even thinking about it, but the fact remained that the vampires had ways of coercing people that humans like us couldn't defend ourselves against no matter how hard we tried.

Estelle gave me a comforting hug. "We'll figure it out."

I looked up as Cass strode into view, a book tucked under her arm. Not one of Aunt Candace's, but the *Vampire Defence* book.

"What's going on?" she asked. "Let me guess—Mortimer Vale told you there are vampires hiding under the desk."

"There *is* a vampire in the basement, as you know perfectly well, but that's not the point," I said. "He seems to think *Laney* is working against us. I wouldn't believe him, but I called her, and she told me those two vampires found her weeks ago to threaten her over my dad's journal, which led to her finding her way here."

"I knew it," she said. "I knew there was something wrong with her story."

"Hold on," I said. "You just implied Mortimer Vale was probably talking nonsense—"

"I implied he's a manipulator, but that doesn't mean he was wrong about your friend," she said. "It made logical sense for her to end up in this world via the vampires. More than her randomly stumbling across our location on the internet."

"Is that why you were so rude to her?"

"Well, yes," said Cass. "She just walked in and accepted

it all. I'd have bet my wand on her being a vampire's plaything. It's their way—they give you a taste, and you want more."

I looked at the book she had tucked underneath her arm. "Have you been reading all about vampires, then?"

"Sure." She shrugged. "Know your enemy. Didn't you read the part about human subjugates?"

"I did," I said slowly. "Aunt Adelaide mentioned that humans who drink vampire blood can be influenced into doing their bidding."

"You think she was hypnotised into taking the journal rather than taking it of her own free will?" Cass said. "Possibly, but I'm more inclined to think she took it to prove her obedience to her vampire master."

"She doesn't have a vampire master." My head spun in circles, and nausea rose in my throat. "I just spoke to her on the phone and she seemed clear-headed enough."

"It's part of the act, isn't it?" said Cass. "Normals make the best targets. Once they've had a little of a vampire's blood, there's nothing they won't do for them."

I shook my head. I wanted to deny it. Every word. I should have kept Laney away from those vampires—but it was too late for regret. And I didn't believe for a minute that she'd willingly hurt me.

Aunt Adelaide walked into the lobby. "What are you all doing here? Is something wrong?"

"The journal's missing again," I said. "Mortimer Vale is accusing Laney of working with the vampires."

"She *is* working with them," said Cass. "It's the only explanation that makes sense."

"I'm not leaving her to them," I said pointedly. "Whether she has the journal or not. She's human."

It was pure luck that those two vampires had come after me first and not her... but that didn't mean they wouldn't try to use her to get at me again. Especially if they figured out that I'd come back to Ivory Beach without her.

"So?" Cass said. "If she wants to be a vampire's chew toy, it's her choice."

"It isn't," I said. "Not if she was coerced."

Whatever the case, I had to find her before those vampires did. She was my friend, and I wouldn't abandon her again.

Aunt Adelaide's gaze clouded. "You know where to find her?"

"I know where she lives, but that's assuming the vampires didn't go after her the instant I came back here." I did my best to shove down the panic brewing in my chest. "I can't waste any more time."

Xavier turned to me. "Are you sure about this?"

"No," I said. "But it's been too long already. If Mortimer Vale lied and he did have a way to contact his fellow vampires, they might be on her tail already."

"Then I'll go with you," he said. "When you're ready."

"We'll hold the fort here in the library," said Estelle. "The moment you find her, bring her straight here."

"I will," I said. "If I'm not back in an hour—"

"Half an hour," said Estelle. "I'll come after you. I remember the way."

"Okay." I turned to Xavier and pulled out my Biblio-Witch Inventory, tapping on the word *travel*.

At once, we fell against one another as the world lurched away... and then we stood on the same bridge as before.

"I really need to pick a better spot to land in." I caught my balance against Xavier's shoulder. "Okay. She lives this way…"

I crossed the bridge, Xavier following on swift Reaper steps. My path faltered when I caught sight of Abe's shop. The windows were darkened, but the door lay slightly open. Weird. Abe should have gone home by now, unless he'd stayed behind to clean or something.

A sweeping wind gusted towards me from behind. I rotated on the spot, and my heart plummeted. Xavier had vanished into thin air, disappearing as though he'd never been there in the first place. Had he seen something and used his swift Reaper speed to intercept it? Or had his boss noticed him sneaking off with me and dragged him back home? I hovered on the spot, debating whether to head back to check up on him, then movement drew my gaze to the shop window again.

My blood iced over. Two figures moved within the shop, too fast to be human. Not Xavier. The door opened, and the vampires' shadowy forms melted into view.

"Hello, Aurora," said the raspy voice of the hat-wearing vampire from earlier.

"What the—?" I peered behind them into the shop. "Where is Abe? What did you do with him?"

"He's at home, of course," said the taller vampire. "We're here to take care of some important business."

"You shouldn't be in here." I reached for my pocket, but they were still inside the shop, and I didn't dare throw firedust inside the doorway in case it set the whole place on fire. The vampires wore identical grins, as though recalling how they'd nearly set the shop ablaze at our first meeting.

They hadn't come back for Laney after all. Unless they were saving that for later. What did they want with Abe's shop? Did they really think my dad had left anything behind?

"Going to use your fire magic, are you?" The taller vampire laughed. "Is it worth destroying the place where you spent your whole childhood?"

My fists clenched. "Get out of my head."

"We don't need to get into your head, Aurora," said his companion. "Your little friend has already told us everything."

No. You're lying. "She didn't. You read her thoughts."

"Same difference." The first vampire gave another laugh. "Are you here to show us where your father hid the means of translating his journal?"

They were serious. They really thought there was a translation document hidden in here. Which was absurd. Abe would have known. *I* would have. I'd spent years looking for a way to translate the journal, because Abe kept threatening to throw it away, telling me it was worthless without a translation. Besides, there was no reason for them to wait until now to come back.

"Give it back," I warned them. "Or I *will* throw the fire-dust at you."

The second vampire raised an eyebrow at my vehemence. "So there *is* a document?"

"No, there isn't," I said. "I meant the journal. And if you ever set foot near my best friend again, then I'll make you sorry."

The two of them exchanged glances. "We don't have the journal. Are you saying you let someone else steal it from you?"

They might not have it, but they weren't budging, either. As long as they remained here in Abe's shop, using fire or water against them was out of the question—but how could I drive them away without putting Laney in danger?

"So your little friend took the journal for herself?" said the taller vampire. "She did our work for us. Now all we need is the translation."

The shorter vampire moved in a blur, catching me by the arm before I could grab my wand. My feet flew off the ground, and I scrambled for my pocket in desperation. My finger traced down the page of my Biblio-Witch Inventory, pinpointing the word *light*.

Brightness flared, but hands ripped the book from my hands and flung it aside. Another pair of hands shoved into my pockets, roughly, as I was hauled into the shop and out of the light.

Then a trapdoor opened, and the vampires threw me down into the darkness.

14

I landed on my arm. Hard. Pain shot up to my shoulder, and I bit back a scream. The brightness of the spell faded, but not before I felt the absence of my Biblio-Witch Inventory in my pocket. They'd taken it —and my wand, too.

"Hey!" I yelled up through the narrow trapdoor above my head. It was pitch black down here, and it didn't help that the shop had no lights on, either. I hadn't been into the basement in years, but Abe had seen no need to install proper stairs and had instead lowered a ladder into the basement every time I needed to get something from down here.

Of course, right now, the ladder was gone. The vampires hadn't wanted to leave me a way out. Nobody even knew I was here except for my family, but they thought I was going after Laney. I reached into my pocket for my phone, but the odds of my message reaching them quickly were almost zero.

Instead, I rose to my feet and reached up with my uninjured arm, but my hand didn't even touch the edge of the trapdoor. I was well and truly stuck. Worse, the vampires ha taken my pen as well as my Biblio-Witch Inventory. If another writing instrument lay down here in the darkness, I couldn't see it. I crouched down and felt around with my uninjured hand, but I found nothing more than concrete floor and a couple of boxes of books.

The sound of the door closing made my head snap up. "What are you doing?"

Nobody replied. Had they seriously abandoned me in here? I'd be in trouble if Abe found me in the morning, but that was nothing to the danger Laney would be in if the vampires went after her next. Whether she had the journal or not.

What were you thinking? I might want to trust my best friend, but I couldn't ignore the evidence any longer, and Alice's words about seeing her outside the library the night of Evangeline's party were the final straw. I didn't know what to believe anymore.

Just when I was debating screaming in the hopes that passers-by might hear me, the shop door creaked open, accompanied by the sound of a familiar voice shouting my name. *Laney.*

"Laney!" I yelled. "I'm down here!"

"And she'll be joining you," said the vampire's voice.

There was a muffled thud and a yelp, and then Laney tumbled head over heels through the trapdoor. I hastened to catch her, only for her to topple onto my injured arm. My vision turned white, and a stifled cry escaped me.

"Ow!" She groaned and shifted position. "Oh, no. Rory. I'm sorry. Are you okay?"

"I will be if you get off my arm," I squeaked out.

She disentangled herself from me, glaring at the vampires' silhouettes peering down at us. "What do you think you're playing at?"

"The two of you are as bad as each other, so we decided to take care of you both at once," said the taller vampire. "You'll stay there until one of you tells me where the journal is. If I can convince you to spill the details on the translation, too, then you might get out faster."

Wait. Laney didn't have the journal after all? Hope flared, swiftly banished beneath a rush of guilt and fear. I'd got us both captured for no reason at all.

"I don't know." I pushed to my knees, my arm throbbing. "I told you. You can tear this place apart and you won't find a thing."

"Then we'll gladly do so," said the second vampire in his raspy voice.

"Get out!" Laney yelled. "Or I swear I'll scream loud enough to bring the police running here. I don't have the journal, idiots."

"Nobody's coming to save you, sweetheart," the first vampire purred. "Scream all you like."

Laney screamed curses at him in answer. I, however, was too occupied by the throbbing pain in my arm to put up much of an argument. Equally painful was the guilt squeezing my chest. I couldn't believe how badly I'd misjudged the situation.

Eventually, Laney sank into a sitting position, putting her head in her hands.

"I'm sorry." I winced at the sound of one of the vampires knocking something over in the shop. "This is my fault. I lost the journal and then I thought they'd go after you. Not come here."

"The journal." She shifted position, revealing the inside pocket of her coat. "You mean this one?"

My eyes bugged out. "You…" I held my breath, but the vampires didn't seem to have heard us. "How?"

By 'how', I meant, *how did you resist the vampires' mind-reading?* They should have known right away that Laney had the journal, especially if she hadn't been holding the protective charm when they'd found her.

"Long story," she muttered. "I took it to keep them from targeting you. Before I went to visit you, I heard they planned to go to the library next. That's why I showed up when I did, but they must have changed their plans."

"Laney." I dropped my voice to a whisper. "Why didn't you tell me?"

"I didn't want to tell you over the phone in case you followed me here." She hung her head. "I planned to put it back when the coast was clear. I'm taking a potion that stops them from reading my thoughts, so I figured they wouldn't guess I had it."

A potion that blocks mind-reading. "Sorry," I whispered back. "It was my thoughts they read. What happened to the protective charm my aunt gave you?"

"I left it behind." She grimaced. "They called me out of my house by telling me they'd kill you if I didn't come with them."

Anger stirred within me, but I pushed it down. If the vampires had the faintest idea what we were saying, we'd lose our last hope of getting out of this in one piece. Even having the journal back didn't change the fact that I couldn't use magic to get us out of here, and if the vampires got hold of it, I'd lose the only advantage I had.

It came as a small comfort that I now knew with certainty that the vampires *didn't* know how to translate it. If they did, they wouldn't be nosing around here looking for a translation document.

I kept my voice low. "They threw my Biblio-Witch Inventory and wand somewhere out there in the shop. They stole my pen, too. If I have pen and paper in my hands, I might be able to use magic to get us out of here, but I'm not sure I can take out both vamps at once."

"I don't have any pens or paper on me." Laney swore under her breath. "They're really intent on searching the place, aren't they? Do they think they're more likely to find that translator thingy here than in the library?"

"Looks that way," I muttered. "They're going to end up disappointed. If anything, my dad probably wrote the translation down on a piece of paper that Abe threw in the bin or something."

All the same, I couldn't help wondering if they were onto something. What if the translation *was* magically hidden? I hadn't known I was a witch until the vampires had walked into my life, but I hadn't been back to the bookshop since that day, nor had I thought to search it for anything magical. If my dad had suspected I might find my way to the magical world, then maybe… maybe he *had* left me a way to translate the journal.

Even if not, this might be my only shot at getting us both out of here in one piece. I leaned in to whisper to Laney, who nodded once, twice. Then I stood up and tilted my head back to look into the darkened shop. The quiet sounds of the vampires searching the shelves rustled in the background.

"Hey," I called up to them. "Hey! I have something to tell you."

The tall vampire's shadow fell over the open trapdoor. "What? This had better be good."

"I know how to find the translation." I did my best to keep my thoughts focused on the dark shop so my lie wouldn't creep through. "My dad left it here for me to find after I entered the magical world. It's hidden in the shop, but it's only accessible to me."

"Rubbish," rasped the second vampire. "You're lying."

"Abe hasn't found it in all the years he's worked here," I told them. "Because my dad didn't want him to. Even I didn't know he hid anything here, but now I'm part of the magical world, I understand. He wants me to find it myself. Nobody else can."

The vampires exchanged whispers. Then the first one hissed, "What if it's true? We've looked behind every shelf. This is a mundane place, not magical at all. There are only so many corners to search."

"This is a trick," said his partner. "She wants us to get her out so she can attack us."

"I'm pretty sure you broke my arm," I told them. "I'm not in any shape to fight you. I just want to get out of here and go home, and so does Laney."

"Fine," snarled the first vampire. "But you're not leaving my sight."

In one smooth motion, he jumped into the basement, grabbed me around the waist, and leapt out the trapdoor again, placing me on the ground.

"Hey!" Laney said. "You can't leave me down here."

"You can stay put," the second vampire rasped. "To guarantee that your little friend does exactly as she promised."

"Along with these." The vampire who'd carried me held up my Biblio-Witch Inventory, pen and wand in his hands. My fists clenched, prompting another bolt of pain up my shoulder. All I had was the journal in my pocket... which might give me away at any moment if they saw past the surface layer of my thoughts.

I had to figure this one out, and fast. Where might my dad have hidden a translation document? If I made the wrong move, I'd meet an ugly end at the vampires' hands —and I couldn't forget Laney, imprisoned down in the darkness.

I'll get her out.

I went to the desk first. It was the same as ever, minus the book which had helped send the vampires away the first time around. I still remembered the title. *The Beginner's Guide to Horticulture.* Had Abe moved it, or had the vampires?

The taller vampire intercepted me when I reached for the light switch on the wall. "Not so fast."

"I can't look for anything when I can't see where I'm going," I protested. "If you aren't going to let me have my wand, at least let me have that."

He grumbled under his breath. "Human senses are so pathetic. Fine, but no funny business. That clear?"

I switched on the light and scanned the shop again. While the light dispelled some of the shadows, the vampires were right about the relative lack of hiding places. If my dad had wanted me to be the one to find the translation, where would he know I'd look?

I made my way among the shelves, looking for any traces of magic, biblio-witchy or otherwise. The two vampires shadowed my every move, as I'd expected, which forced me to move slower than I'd have liked. The pain in my arm didn't help either. I couldn't think clearly —which should at least make my thoughts more difficult to read.

"What's taking you so long?" said the first vampire. "You're going too slow."

"It's well-hidden," I said. "Have some patience, won't you?"

I moved down the row, scanning titles until I came across the non-fiction section. There, I sought out the section on gardening books, careful to keep my thoughts clear of my real plan.

There it was. *The Beginner's Guide to Horticulture* stood at the end of a row, as though Abe had shoved it away after my departure. I had no idea if the spell was still active, but I eased it off the shelf. All at once, it began to glow with a golden light, the same way it had when I'd first touched it.

"What's that?" asked the vampire sharply, leaning over my shoulder. "You found it?"

I swung the book around and hit him in the face. As he stumbled back, stunned, I yanked my wand out of his hand and cast the freeze-frame spell. As both vampires froze on the spot, I grabbed my Biblio-Witch Inventory and pen from his hand, too. Then I shoved them into my pocket, fumbling with my one good hand as I ran to the trapdoor into the basement.

The instant I reached it, the shop door flew open, and

Aunt Adelaide ran in, accompanied by Estelle. The book's spell had called them here.

The vampires unfroze, but I spun around and freeze-framed them again. Then I used my wand to levitate Laney out of the trapdoor. She yelped and flailed, catching her balance against the desk when I lowered her to the ground.

"Sorry," I whispered. "This is awkward—"

The vampires unfroze, only for Aunt Adelaide to step in and wave her own wand. The vampires flew into the air, rotating like spinning tops.

"Unhand us at once!" rasped the shorter vamp, who'd lost his hat somewhere in the shop.

"You're breaking and entering," said Aunt Adelaide. "For what purpose are you tormenting my niece and an innocent normal?"

Estelle stepped to her mother's side. "Let me guess… this is about Rory's dad's journal."

"What else?" said the taller vampire. "We almost had the means of translating it in our hands, but the girl deceived us."

"Of course she did," Aunt Adelaide said with pride in her voice. "You didn't think we'd have left the bookshop unprotected, did you? You're coming with us."

Estelle took over, levitating the struggling vampires towards the door. "They deserve to join Mortimer Vale behind bars, don't you think, Rory?"

"They do," I agreed. "I need to check something first, but I'll be with you in a second."

I might have planned to deceive the vampires, but perhaps there *was* something in here which would point to where my dad's translation was hidden. Besides, it wouldn't do to leave the shop in such a mess, even if I didn't work here any longer.

"If you need us, you know how to call us back," said Estelle.

And without further ado, she and her mother vanished along with the two vampires.

"Whoa," said Laney. "Nice going."

"I'm glad Abe didn't throw out that book." I scanned the darkened shop. "I know it's a long shot, but I don't have any other ideas about the missing translation. Why didn't I think of looking here before?"

More to the point, why did I still feel a nagging doubt that I'd overlooked something obvious? Okay, the vampires were on their way to jail, but they'd still barged into my old life and left a trail of chaos behind. Abe was going to think someone had broken in, but it was better that he didn't know who'd really been responsible.

Laney moved to help me put some of the books back on the shelf, while I scanned every corner for any sign of my dad's translation document. Whatever it looked like. If it was hidden in a book, Abe might have moved it a dozen times in the years since his death.

"Uh, can't you use magic to find it?" asked Laney.

I hit myself in the forehead with my free hand. "Right. Yeah. I'm going to blame that one on my broken arm."

She grinned, while I pulled out my Biblio-Witch Inventory and skipped to the very first word I'd written in it—*find*.

I pressed my fingertip to the word, focusing on the journal in my pocket as hard as I could, and envisioning a piece of paper, a book, a note.

A faint orange glow from a shelf near the back of the

shop caught my attention. I approached, crouching to examine the lowest shelf. A book lay there, and underneath it, a piece of paper glowed faintly. I picked it up, my gaze drinking in the lines of familiar symbols.

"Very good," said Mortimer Vale. "Now, hand it to me."

15

I rotated on the spot, hardly breathing. Mortimer Vale stood in the shop doorway, looking between Laney and me. "If you're wondering if you were in part responsible for my presence here, you're mistaken. I've been engineering my escape from that cell ever since I found myself unfortunate enough to end up behind bars. A miscalculation on my part, but not one I intend to repeat."

"It's too late for your two friends," I told him. "They're already on their way to jail. You can't pretend *that* was part of your plan."

"They're resourceful. They'll find a way out, I don't doubt." He moved in a blur and appeared right in front of me, a hand outstretched. "Give me the journal and the document, or things will get very unpleasant for you."

"I won't." I went for my Biblio-Witch Inventory instead, and he grabbed me with swift hands. A bookshelf collapsed when I flung myself around the corner out of the way, shoving the document into my pocket as I did so.

That made it easier to hit the word *light* with my fingertips, igniting a white glow which forced the vampire to cover his eyes.

Laney sprang up behind and hit him over the head with a book. "Take that, you evil old bloodsucker."

Mortimer's outstretched hand knocked Laney head over heels. I shouted her name, but she recovered, bracing herself against a bookshelf.

I cast the freeze-frame spell, missed, and Mortimer Vale tackled me. The resulting jolt of pain up my injured arm nearly made me pass out. "You don't have to make this difficult for yourself, Aurora. Your friend has already made enemies of my kind when she slaughtered them. If I were less merciful, I would kill her in turn."

My breath rushed out. "You *what?*"

He held me effortlessly, pinning down my wand arm. "I'm not lying, Aurora. I did wonder, when I heard of the recent deaths, if another rogue had found their way to town. Of course it makes much more sense that they would have sent your friend in their place. They knew you trusted her without exception, and they knew you wouldn't suspect her."

I shook my head. No way. She couldn't have. Laney wasn't a killer. She might have taken the journal, but she'd done so to protect me, nothing more.

"They even gave her a potion to stop other vampires from reading her thoughts," he said. "Very few have access to that, except for other Founders. When I find out who put her up to it, they'll die, of course, but you won't be around to see it, Aurora. It's too risky for me to let you live."

"You're lying," I choked out.

"He isn't," Laney said from behind him. "I killed them, just like I'm going to kill him."

She threw herself at the vampire, a sharpened wooden stake in her hand. He let go of me with a snarl, avoiding the blow. I lay there for an instant, stunned, reeling with the impact of her words. *Laney.* No, it was impossible.

And yet… someone had given Laney a potion to block vampires' mind-control. She'd evaded them for this long. Did I really know what she was capable of?

I rose to my feet and cast the freeze-frame spell, halting the vampire mid-step. My arm throbbed, my mind ticking over all the possible ways to subdue him. In the end, I had only one solution. I went for my Biblio-Witch Inventory, tapping the word *travel* and envisioning the inside of the jail in Ivory Beach with everything I had.

At once, all three of us vanished from the bookshop and reappeared on the seafront, down the road from the pier. The spell had brought us close to the jail—but not close enough.

Mortimer Vale recovered first, recognising our surroundings, and broke into a run. His dark figure blurred and vanished from sight in the direction of the town square.

"Dammit!" I ran after him, Laney on my heels, but the guy moved too fast. His companions ought to be in jail by now, but that didn't mean he'd come quietly after tasting freedom again.

"I thought he really wanted that journal," Laney said breathlessly from behind me.

"He does. I bet he's going after my family." I quickened my pace, the chill air battering at my face. "Probably thinks he can use them as leverage to threaten me into handing over the journal and the translation."

"Evil man." Laney overtook me, outpacing me with enough ease to make me wonder how I'd missed the signs. She might look and sound the same as ever, but there was an elegance to the way she moved which hadn't been there before, and she still clutched the stake in her hand. "Rory, I can explain—"

"We can talk about it later."

I couldn't think about my best friend as a killer, not now. Not when I had to ensure my family members were safe from harm. I sprinted across the square, spotting the fleeing vampire reach the library steps. He gave me a mocking wave, then the door closed behind him.

I swore and ran faster. Even so, Laney reached the library first and pulled open the door to reveal the empty lobby. I tensed in the doorway, certain of a trap, and sure enough...

"I'm glad you're here, Aurora," said the now-hatless vampire in his raspy voice.

His taller companion appeared on the other side of the door, joined by Mortimer Vale. All three vampires surrounded Laney and me, their fangs bared in grins.

"What did you do with my family?" I demanded.

Sylvester was supposed to be watching the place. Jet, too. But even they would have trouble dealing with three vampires at once.

"Nothing permanent," said the taller vampire. "Nobody has to get hurt, Aurora."

"You made a mistake coming here," I said. "This is my family's home, and the library protects us."

The three vamps closed in, moving fast enough for

their bodies to blur. I leapt onto the desk and yelled, "Sylvester! Jet! Spark!"

At once, Sylvester dove from the ceiling like a feathery bullet, crashing into one of the vampires before his hands could touch me. My hunch had been right. The vampires might have shoved my family out of the way, but they wouldn't have thought to look for our familiars.

"You ruined my nap!" yelled Sylvester. He pecked furiously at the vampire, forcing him to raise his hands over his head to protect himself.

As for me, I grabbed my Biblio-Witch Inventory and jabbed the word *move!*

The shelves rumbled forward, enclosing the vampires on all sides. Books fell to the floor or took flight, pages snapping at them and adding to the clamour.

Mortimer Vale cast me a murderous glance and leapt high, dodging the moving shelves and slamming into me. Once again, I found myself on my back, my wand hand pinned down and my injured arm screaming with pain.

"Get away from her!" Laney jumped on him from behind. He snarled and let go of me, trying to dislodge her, but she hung on, tenacious. The owl circled the vampires, pecking furiously, and Jet joined him with a loud screech.

"Partner!" he yelled.

"I could use a hand," I called to him. Mortimer finally broke away from me, dislodging Laney, only for Spark to fly into his face like a glittery wasp. He yelled in fury, hitting out blindly at the pixie flitting around his head.

I climbed to my feet and directed the shelves to move around the vampires once again, but they dodged, too fast to enclose their prey. If only I could trap them in a basement like they'd done to me… *That's an idea.*

I thought fiercely of the basement and jabbed the word *move* one last time.

No sooner had the thought crossed my mind than a trapdoor opened beneath the vampires' feet. One of them fell in with a snarl of fury, but the others danced aside with swift-footed grace, shielding themselves from the aerial assault of the library's three familiars.

Mortimer Vale recovered first, but the bookshelves shunted him backwards. The vampire tripped over his own feet and toppled through the open trapdoor into the basement, pulling his companion along with him. A muffled yelp and a thud followed. I ran over and slammed the lid before hitting *lock* in my Biblio-Witch Inventory. *That ought to hold them.*

"Where—" I caught my breath, watching the three familiars descend to join me. "Where are the others?"

"Locked inside the Vampire Section upstairs," said Sylvester. "I was trying to get the door open when you came back."

"Glad you came to help." I was, too. Sylvester might be cantankerous and fond of holding a grudge, but he'd always step in to protect the library. "Uh—the *Vampire* Section? How'd they end up in there?"

"When Cass went looking for more books on defending oneself against the undead, a certain book wraith escaped," he said. "She decided to deal with the creature herself, with obvious consequences."

"And my aunts went to help her?" I guessed. "Then how'd the vampires get out of jail?"

"From what I surmised, Edwin had to deal with a

sudden and horrendous outbreak of wild rats," he said. "Your aunts left the vampires in the care of the prison guards, but when they returned to protect the library…"

"The vampires came here and locked them upstairs," I finished. "Mortimer Vale was already gone. He came after me. And… and I guess he orchestrated the whole escape plan. Is Edwin okay?"

"How am I supposed to know?" the owl huffed. "I'm only useful as target practise, apparently."

"Don't be ridiculous," I said to him. "You just saved my neck. Laney, too."

Laney groaned. Mortimer had tossed her aside when he'd broken her grip, and she wore a slightly dazed expression on her face which turned to wariness when she caught me looking. "Rory…"

My breath caught in my throat, while the pain in my arm began to return in full force now the adrenaline had worn off. But we had to have this conversation at some point. Before I lost my nerve.

"You staked those vampires?" I asked. "For real? Did one of the vampires force you, or…?"

"Oh, Rory." She sat upright. "I'm sorry. I didn't know how to tell you, but I didn't kill them on anyone's orders. I did it for you."

"What do you mean?" Disbelief rooted me to the spot as a dozen questions cascaded through my mind.

The library door opened, and Xavier strode in, his scythe out and his expression as grim as his namesake.

"Rory." He swept over to me. "I'm sorry I left you. Someone died at the jail when we were leaving town. My boss insisted on accompanying me to deal with the situation. If he'd known I intended to leave town, he'd never have let me help you. Where are the vampires?"

"They killed someone during the escape?" Maybe Mortimer Vale had done so intentionally to draw Xavier away. The evil man. I pointed to the trapdoor with my uninjured hand, and Sylvester landed on top of it with his wings spread out. "The vampires are in there. Can you let Edwin know? I need to let my family out of the upstairs corridor the vamps locked them in."

"Sure." He gave me a quick hug, tensing when I winced. "You're hurt."

"Later," I insisted. "Quickly. I don't know how long the trapdoor will hold them."

"Forever, if I have anything to do with it," Sylvester said. "I wouldn't trust those security trolls an inch if they can be scared off by a swarm of rodents."

"The vampires will be going somewhere more secure this time, I don't doubt," Xavier said darkly. "All three of them. I'll make sure of it."

He left the library, swift and silent. I, meanwhile, made for the stairs to the first floor, from which a loud banging noise issued.

Laney trod behind me. "Rory, I understand if you don't want to talk to me again, but I just want you to know why I did it."

I reached the top of the stairs and turned to her. "I'm having a lot of trouble wrapping my head around this, to be honest. And I don't want to say anything I'll regret."

"Do you still have the journal?" Her eyes went to my pocket. "I never wanted to steal it, but the vampires were utterly obsessed with it. After they cornered me and asked if I knew about it, they gave me an invitation to a big event of theirs and promised I wouldn't be the only human there. I worried they'd be plotting your murder or something, so... so I went."

I tensed. "And were they?"

"Pretty much." She rubbed her eyes, which were damp. "I mean, they were plotting ways to get the journal and most of them ended up with you dead. But some of them were also plotting to break a member of their group out of jail."

"Rudolph Mint," I said. "He came to Ivory Beach..."

"To kill you." Tears ran from her eyes. "I couldn't see another way around it. I barely knew what I was doing, but—"

"You fought a *vampire?*" I shook my head. "But you're—"

"Human, but I drank their blood," she said. "I had to drink it at the party to blend in—and besides, it came with a few nifty advantages. A human who drinks their blood temporarily becomes as strong and fast as a vamp. I also had that potion which blocks mind-reading, so he didn't sense me creeping up on him."

"So you killed him," I said. "And then... you came to the town the night of Evangeline's party, too. Alice from the pet shop said she saw you trying to get into the library."

"To warn you, of course," she said. "I tried the doors, then it occurred to me that you might be at the gathering, too. The second vampire who died was planning to ambush you on the way out of the party. Afterwards, I hoped that if I took the journal off you, they'd stop trying. I wasn't sure how much you knew."

A hand clenched around my heart. "I can't hate you for

that, Laney. I don't blame you either. I'm just… shocked. Nothing is how I thought it was."

"I know the feeling." She rubbed her eyes again. "But I really hope we can still stay friends."

"Of course we can." I'd known her for too long, and now we'd been through too much together for me to think we weren't in with a shot of fixing this. "Everything's going to be fine."

She hugged me. "Of course it is."

I made a muffled noise when she accidentally knocked my injured arm. Something damp brushed my face. "Ow. Not if I don't fix this arm, too. Also, I think I'm bleeding, or one of us is."

Laney let go of me, her hand going to her neck. Two bite marks stood out against her pale skin.

Oh, no.

16

I hovered outside the door of the guest room, waiting for news on Laney's condition, my nerves thrumming.

Once I'd set my family free from the Vampire Section, my aunts had snapped into action. My broken arm had been fixed in a heartbeat, but Laney was a different story. Normally, the bite wouldn't have done any lasting damage, but she'd drank vampire blood at least twice when she'd met up with the vampires, which gave her a higher-than-average chance of going through the trans-formation process. For that reason, we'd let her stay in a guest room overnight.

Then she hadn't woken up. For three days and counting.

Aunt Adelaide paid frequent visits with various potions and spells to see if she could help, but even magic couldn't reverse a vampire transformation in progress. All we could do was wait for Laney to wake.

"Hey, Rory." Estelle hugged me on the way past her room. "Don't blame yourself."

"How did you—"

"I know you," she said. "You did everything you could."

I made an indistinct noise. I'd done my best, yet it hadn't been enough. My family knew Laney had killed the two vampires, but not whether Evangeline would find out or what to do if she did. The leader of the vampires hadn't been a friend of the victims, but that didn't change the fact that Laney had killed two vamps on her territory, and the potion blocking vampires from reading her mind would have worn off by the time she awoke. "I know. I should find a hobby or something."

The only thing distracting me from Laney's plight was the journal, but the translator spell would take several days to learn the code from the document I'd found in Abe's shop and then apply it to each page of the journal. That left me with entirely too much brain space to worry about my best friend, the vampires, and our future.

"The journal's translation should be ready soon, my mum said," added Estelle, as though she'd sensed the direction of my thoughts. "But the pile of returns is getting a little high."

"Sorry. I've been distracted." I turned my back on Laney's room and made my way to the stairs, crossing my fingers that she'd wake soon.

Mortimer Vale and his friends had been jailed, but that didn't change the fact that Laney had left a trail of enemies behind her. If anyone else found out she'd killed two members of the Founders' group, they might target her, too.

But she wouldn't be undefended. Not as long as she had me.

I walked into the lobby and spotted an all-too-familiar figure waiting for me, as though conjured up by my thoughts.

Evangeline watched me approach her without speaking. Then she said, "Your friend should have reported that vampire to me."

"Which vampire?" I hadn't the faintest idea what she was talking about.

"Lord Datherel," she said. "The vampire who met an unfortunate end at my party. If she'd told me he was plotting against you rather than taking matters into her own hands, then I wouldn't be facing this dilemma."

She knew. She'd worked out the truth without even reading our thoughts. *She visited Mortimer Vale and his friends. I should have known.*

"Which dilemma?" My voice sounded smaller than usual. "Laney is in a coma."

"And she killed two vampires," she said. "Ordinarily, I'd punish that crime by exiling her from town, but since the perpetrator was human..."

My throat closed up. "Laney was only trying to protect me. She was drinking vampire blood at the time, too, which might have messed with her head."

"Infuriating," she muttered. "Most of my people would want her driven out of town or put to death, but I'm sure you've gathered by now that I do not share that opinion."

My heart kicked against my ribs. "You don't?"

"It is not my wish to exile a new vampire before she has the chance to prove herself to me," she said.

Of course there'd be a catch. I couldn't picture Laney

being enthused at the notion of joining up with Evange-line any more than the Founders. "I don't even know if Laney is going to choose to stay here in the magical world. I wouldn't blame her if she didn't."

"You want her to stay, do you not?"

"It's not my choice to make." My voice rose with unexpected anger. "It's hers. It doesn't count if bribery is involved, or coercion, or anything. I'm not going to let you blackmail or bully her into joining you, and if you keep ignoring how your fellow vampires treat humans, there'll be more incidents like this."

Her eyes flared with restrained rage. "The other vampires will not agree. We cannot police every single one of our own, especially when they flaunt the law in areas outside of our usual jurisdiction."

"Even so, you know the members of the Founders, don't you?" I said. "It can't be hard to keep tabs on them, considering all the resources you have. If you'd been watching, you'd have known some of them would come to your party with the intention of causing me harm."

I knew I'd pay for needling her, but the fact remained that Laney had killed the two vampires to protect me, and if Evangeline had been aware of their existence, then she might have been able to prevent her from taking that step. It wasn't like Evangeline couldn't have read the minds of her fellow vampires to determine which ones posed a threat to me or to other humans. She was just used to not having to do anything to stop her fellow vampires from threatening those she considered beneath her.

Another flicker of anger passed across her face, but she said nothing to deny that she'd heard my thoughts. I'd had time enough to consider how she might have intervened over the last few days, and every time, I landed on the conclusion that doing nothing hadn't been her only option. Better than leaving a defenceless human to take matters into her own hands and face the consequences which should have fallen on the vampires themselves.

When she spoke, it was in a stiff, formal tone. "If your friend wishes to see me, you know where to find me."

She left at a swift glide, disappearing through the library doors.

I breathed out as she did so. *That was a close one.*

"Her again," said Cass from behind the desk. "I'm guessing we're going to be seeing a lot more of her."

"Not if I can help it," I said. "If she tries to recruit Laney, there's going to be trouble."

"I think your friend knows better," Cass commented.

I raised an eyebrow. "I think that's the first positive thing I've ever heard you say about her."

"I never said she was wrong in what she did," said Cass. "I've imagined staking some of those creepy vamps a dozen times. But she's not been involved in our world long enough to see the long-term consequences of that. *Really* long-term, if she goes full vamp."

Right. Vampires were immortal and never aged—another new reality Laney would have to deal with whether she stayed here or not.

I pushed the thought aside to deal with later. "I'm not so sure the vamps are good at seeing long-term consequences, either. Did they really think they could get away with trapping all of you inside our own library? Did one of *them* set the book wraith loose?"

"No," she said, "but it might have heard the ruckus

from the jail. Your vampire friend made every rodent in town come to the surface to obey his commands."

"He's not my friend," I said. "I'd be more than happy to let him rot in jail for the rest of his life."

"We'll see how that works out." She shrugged. "Was the journal worth it, then?"

"It's still in the translator spell," I told her.

"Better read it before Evangeline comes back," she said. "If she hasn't already got her paws on it."

"She hasn't," said a voice. Sylvester sat on a shelf, looking down at the pair of us. He'd still been avoiding me most of the time, but he'd thankfully refrained from commenting on Laney's situation. "It's nearly ready. I think you should throw a party to celebrate, given how much trouble it's caused you."

"Are you just asking for more balloons to destroy?" I rolled my eyes. "Wasn't pecking those vampires enough?"

Jet and the pixie flew overhead, chasing one another. Sylvester tutted at both of them.

"I'm the only civilised animal in this place," he said.

"Yes, you are," said Cass. "Tell you what, that book wraith would make a good security guard—"

"Don't you even think about it," I said. "Let me guess— you two made friends while you were trapped in the upstairs corridor."

The door opened, thankfully sparing me from having to explain the myriad reasons I didn't want that book wraith anywhere near me. Xavier walked into the library, and Sylvester greeted him by putting on a posh voice and cawing, "Welcome to our humble home."

"Hey." The Reaper arched a brow. "What's the occasion?"

"You," said the owl. "We're throwing you a special Reaper-themed party."

"No, we're not." I shooed him away, and he took flight up to the balcony. Cass withdrew, too, leaving the pair of us alone.

"Honestly." I shook my head after them. "Laney isn't awake yet, by the way."

He'd been checking on me with the same question every few hours ever since she'd fallen into a coma.

"I just wanted to see how you were." Xavier dug his hand into his pocket. "And to give you this."

He pressed a cold, grey stone into my hand. "What's this?"

"A way for you to summon me if I'm not around," he said. "I got the idea from that book you told me about. The one your aunts left in the bookshop where you used to work, which let you call them to your side. Just give it a squeeze, and it'll alert me to your location and enable me to find you."

"Oh." I pocketed the stone. "Good idea. Would it work even if your boss locked you up?"

"He can't lock me up," he said. "But yes, it should work from anywhere, in theory. He'll also flay me with his scythe if he knows I gave it to you."

"Good job he can't read minds, then," I said. "Um, he's not bothered by what Laney did, is he?"

"Why would he be? He doesn't know her."

"Evangeline showed up and dropped a bunch of hints that she's watching the situation," I told him. "She wants Laney to join her horde. Which is unlikely, but I don't know. Her options are on hold until she wakes up, to be honest."

"Rory," Estelle called to me. "She's awake."

I remained rooted to the spot for a moment, and Xavier gave me a quick hug. "Call me if you need me, okay?"

"I will."

Then I was on my way to the stairs, up to the guest room. The door was already open, and inside, Laney sat up in bed. To my surprise, she looked more or less the same. Maybe a little paler than usual, and though her appearance was dishevelled, there was an alertness to the way she moved that hadn't been there beforehand.

Then she sprang up to my side so fast that she nearly knocked me over.

"Rory!" she said. "Wow. You look… different."

"Me?" My eyes followed her newly graceful movements. "Are you okay?"

"Yeah." She blinked. "Whoa. Everything's so bright and intense. I can see every detail. And… god, I'm hungry."

"You want blood?" Estelle passed me a bottle of dark liquid. "The vampires in town take donations from the local blood bank."

"Good, because I haven't wrapped my head around the idea of biting random people yet." Laney took the bottle from me and downed the contents in two gulps. "That's better. Not to creep you out, Rory, but you smell good."

"That was kind of creepy, but I guess it's an occupational hazard of having a vampire's super-senses," I said. "Are you okay, otherwise?"

"I think so." She winced when Estelle entered the room along with Aunt Adelaide. "Ow. Can you… back off a little? I can hear bits of your thoughts at once, and it's giving me a headache."

"Right, of course." Aunt Adelaide indicated to the others to stay back. "Estelle, did you give her the blood?"

"I did," Estelle said. "That ought to be enough for now, but you'll need to feed every few hours at first until your new body adjusts to the change."

"Oh." Laney sat back on the bed, her expression dazed. "I'm going to have to learn how to be a vampire, aren't I? Do you have a guidebook?"

"Usually, the vampire responsible for turning someone is the one who gives them guidance, but since he isn't present at the moment, we're going to have to decide for ourselves." Aunt Adelaide's mouth pressed together. "Laney, if you want to live with Evangeline and her fellow vampires, you can, but there's no guarantee they'll opt to offer you protection after you killed two of their own."

"Oh." She glanced at me. "What's the alternative?"

"You can go home," I said. "The problem with that is your vampire abilities are raw. You'll keep hearing people's thoughts, while your senses will be overwhelming and so will your bloodlust."

"Ugh." She pulled a face. "Pretty sure I've already lost my job by this point, considering I vanished for... how many days has it been?"

"Three," I told her. "I don't know about your job, but I think dealing with customer service as a newly awakened vampire will be tricky. It's up to you, of course."

"I know." She climbed to her feet again. "I have to get used to this whether I stay here or leave. If I go home..."

"If you like, we can give you enough blood supplies to last you for a few weeks, but we can't control anything else that might happen," I said. "Like if the other vampires come after you. You're more than a match for them, but in the normal world…"

"Other people might get hurt." Her gaze shadowed. "The local vampires all live in that church, right?"

"Most of them do, but others live in big fancy mansions on the far side of town," I said. "Granted, they're all filthy rich from being hundreds of years old."

"And I'm flat broke." She wrinkled her nose. "Why are there never any millennial vampires who are still paying off student loans? I can barely afford my rent as it is."

"You can stay here in the library while you get used to being a vampire," I told her. "If you change your mind later, it's fine, but you'll have a roof over your head while you decide whether to stay in the magical world or not."

"Are you sure?" she said.

"Of course I'm sure," I said. "You're my best friend. Not to mention a vampire slayer. I want you where I can keep an eye on you."

She grinned, exposing her new fangs. Once, I might have recoiled at the sight of them, but not now. "Thanks, Rory. I won't cause any more trouble. I'll try not to, anyway."

I had a feeling our vampire-related troubles were just entering a new chapter, but I had my best friend back, the troublesome vampires were jailed, the Founders' plans were thwarted… and my dad's journal translation would be ready for me to read soon enough.

It was almost time for me to find out the rest of my dad's secrets. The road ahead of me might not be an easy one, but Laney and I would face it together.

ABOUT THE AUTHOR

Elle Adams lives in the middle of England, where she spends most of her time reading an ever-growing mountain of books, planning her next adventure, or writing. Elle's books are humorous mysteries with a paranormal twist, packed with magical mayhem.

She also writes urban and contemporary fantasy novels as Emma L. Adams.

Find Elle on Facebook at https://www.facebook.com/pg/ElleAdamsAuthor/